Dalrymple J. Belgrave

Jack Warleigh

A Tale of the Turf and the Law: Vol. II.

Dalrymple J. Belgrave

Jack Warleigh
A Tale of the Turf and the Law: Vol. II.

ISBN/EAN: 9783337082550

Printed in Europe, USA, Canada, Australia, Japan

Cover: Foto ©Andreas Hilbeck / pixelio.de

More available books at **www.hansebooks.com**

BY

DALRYMPLE J. BELGRAVE

IN TWO VOLUMES
VOL. II.

LONDON—CHAPMAN AND HALL

LIMITED

1891

CONTENTS.

JACK WARLEIGH.

CHAPTER I.

IN WHICH TWO OLD ALLIES SEPARATE.

" WELL, and what are we going to do?"
asked Colonel Beamish of the lawyer, as
the Crier's number went up, after the
Grand National.

"Don't know what *you* are going to
do," answered the other, laying a good
deal of stress on the personal pronoun.
"I am going up to town by the next
train, and when I get home, I shall have
a look into matters, see what I have to
settle, and how I can manage it. It seems
to me that our partnership has about come
to an end; and that when the horses are
sold, you will owe me some hundreds."

" I shan't have a penny left, what on
earth shall I do?" said Beamish.

· "You! What do I care what you'll
do.?" answered Lukes. "Our connection is at an end, now that this precious

B

plan of yours has broken down. You'll leave off owing me money, and unless you propose to pay it, I don't want to hear any more of you. What can you do? Why, you can go to the devil."

One or two men who knew that the lawyer had laid very heavily against the Crier, were surprised to see what a good loser he seemed. He was perfectly cool and quiet, though he owned he had backed the second horse for a lot of money, as well as having laid heavily against the winner.

That he must have more money than they ever thought he had, if he could take what he lost so coolly, was the opinion of several men who watched him.

"That sort of bred 'un isn't as a rule a good loser. Perhaps he will go home and cut his throat. I'll take thirty-three to one about his doing it," said Captain Baxter.

"Lay you five hundred to fifty, he's alive in a week's time," answered Sir Peregrine Evergreen. "He won't cut his own throat, if he can make anything by cutting any one else's. Perhaps he had a good race after all. You never can tell with those beggars, they are as artful as can be," answered the other. "I don't think he has though, come to look into his face. I'm not sorry he's

in the wrong box for once. Wonder
what made him lay against the Crier in
the way he did, though? What do you
suppose he thought he knew?"

"Don't know, and I'm not going to
say what I think. It seemed to me, you
couldn't back the horse as soon as it was
known Tom Ring was going to ride it."

Probably Mr. Lukes would not have
kept quite so cool had he not been well
aware that his discomfiture would give
the keenest pleasure to some of his
acquaintances; but the strain was too
great for him to keep up long, and he
was glad when he found himself in a
railway carriage bound for London. He
was not ruined by any means, but he was
very hard hit. Still, he had one thing to
look forward to. Now the race was over,
and he had time to consider the matter in
which he had employed Sam Paradine, it
seemed to him that there was a good
chance of its turning out a profitable
business, and the extreme stress to which
the result of the race would put Cecil
Warleigh, might prove a circumstance
out of which he could make something.
It was going double or quits with a vengeance; if he backed Cecil's claim and
was defeated, he would be ruined. But he
would take care not to do that unless it

looked a sure thing. And if it were a
sure thing, then his kind friends, who
had looked at him so triumphantly just
now in the betting ring, would learn that
Kit Lukes was a long bit from being done
for, and would live to see one or two of
them coming to him praying his assistance
and begging him to give them time.

Colonel Beamish did not take matters so philosophically, nor did it seem
possible for him to see any way out of his
troubles. If he chose to pay, he was dead
broke. He did not take Lukes' advice,
but went to the refreshment bar under
the Grand Stand, and drank glass after
glass of brandy.

That evening there was a row in the
billiard-room of the hotel. The Colonel
was savagely drunk, and he got into a
quarrel with a book-maker to whom he
had lost some money. Before he was
turned out, which was a matter of some
difficulty, he made a little speech to the
assembled company, which afterwards
excited a good deal of comment. First of
all he stated that he was not going to pay
up one penny, and he would see them all
blanked first. He went on to express his
opinion of racing men, from the highest
to the lowest. He then declared his
intention of 'doing' for Mr. Kit Lukes,

and then he gave, to any one who cared
to listen to it, a sketch of the little plot
by which he, Lukes, and Cecil Warleigh,
intended to secure the victory of Blue
Ruin. Having thus done as much mischief as he could, he was induced to
leave.

" That's about the last we shall see of
that gentleman," said Sir Peregrine, who
was present, " but he has taken care that
a good many people shall remember him."

" Wonder if there's anything in what
he said about Warleigh?" answered
Captain Baxter. " If there is, it will
soon be all out. He won't be able to
settle, I suppose."

" I'll take a hundred to twenty that he
doesn't settle. Why was he so keen to
ride with a smashed leg?" answered Sir
Peregrine. " Very plucky of him, some
people say, but it is a precious good thing
for his nephew he didn't. You know
what I told you about the market; this
bears it out, I say. Of course nobody is
going to believe that fellow, only men
will talk, you know, men will talk."

Mr. Lukes arrived at his offices in
Burleigh Street at an early hour next
morning, and with a power of concen-
tration that was very creditable to him,
he put the race for the Grand National

out of his mind altogether. First he had a few words with the expert in hand-writing, whom he had sent down to look at the signature in the register. The man was not a celebrated professor of his art, and seldom or never gave evidence.

" No good, bless yer, ain't got a forensic touch about him. He will never dis-tinguish himself, will that young man," was the verdict passed upon his maiden appearance in a witness box, by Mr. Barrage the great expert in handwriting, to a rival. But though he made rather a poor witness, he had one gift which it has become doubtful whether either of those great men possess to any extent. In seven cases out of ten, he could form a correct opinion as to whether a signature was a forgery or was genuine, and on the three other occasions he was willing to confess himself unable to judge. This was his verdict in the present case.

" Don't know, it's six on one side, and half a dozen on the other. If it was written by a forger, it was one who had practised the signature ever so many times. It somehow half seems to me to be not quite the thing perhaps, but then, when a man is married he is a bit shaky. I don't know what there is wrong about it after all. But there is one thing that I will go bail on. Any one of the men in the front of the business, will pass it as right or go against it as wrong according to who sends 'em to look at it."

Kit Lukes had found occasion to take that man's opinion several times as to points that arose in money-lending business, and he had learned to believe in it.

So far, things looked prosperous, and it seemed that as yet he need not drop Cecil Warleigh, as he had his late partner Colonel Beamish, but on the contrary he hoped a good deal could still he made out of him. It seemed a curious story enough at first sight, but then Kit Lukes had come across some very curious stories in his career as a money-lender and shady lawyer, and had found them to be perfectly true. Everything, so far, had told in favour of the case that might be set up for Cecil Warleigh. Such information as he had gleaned about the character of the late Captain Warleigh, suggested that he had been a man who might have been reckless as to consequences in gratifying any fancy he might have taken. Amongst others, he had made inquiries of Beamish, who, he remembered, had professed to have known him.

"What did you know about this Sir John Warleigh's father?" he had said to his then partner, when they were travelling to Liverpool together.

"I know nothing of him—what are you prying into now? Haven't I told you before to leave the past alone," Beamish had answered, with a look of mistrust and suspicion.

"I don't want to know anything about your dealings with him, so don't fly out like that. What sort of a man was he?"

"Well, he was one of those youngsters whom there is no holding—a sort that seems to be going out nowadays. Would do what he chose, and hang the consequences."

That Captain Warleigh had always had a high reputation as an honourable man, did not greatly affect Lukes. He had taught himself to believe that most men were capable of anything in the way of crime and folly, and that good character meant very little.

All the points of the case so far seemed in his favour. The cheque which had been duly paid by the late Captain Warleigh's bankers would, he thought, in the opinion of nine juries out of ten prove the identity of the man by whom it purported to be drawn.

Yes, on the whole he thought that Cecil Warleigh's claim was good enough for him to take up as his last chance.

CHAPTER II.

On the Monday after the Grand National, Cecil Warleigh's leg was terribly swollen and inflamed, and he was kept in bed by the doctor's orders,—for once he felt very little wish to disobey them. His own rooms seemed a blessed haven of refuge. The servant had orders to say that he was not able to see any one. Cecil could do nothing but let affairs take their course, which must, so far as he could see, lead to his utter smash and ruin. He had no means of settling the heavy bets he had laid against the Crier. Probably, men had already begun to talk, and in a few hours it would be public property that he was a very heavy loser, through the horse he was to have ridden, winning. He had received two letters that morning, one of which irritated, though it half amused him ; the other made him clench his teeth and swear savagely. The former was from young Brookes of the regiment, congratulating him on the Crier's victory, condoling with him on the accident which had prevented him from riding, and thanking him for his advice by which the writer had profited ; the other was written by Jack Warleigh, who seemed in a state of gushing happiness—telling him that he had proposed to Kate Cottingham and had been accepted.

Yes, Jack was in luck. He had all he wanted, and yet perhaps he would not be so deliriously happy if he learnt all that Cecil could tell him about the girl he was engaged to. He was startled from this train of thought, by a knock at the door, and the arrival of about the last visitor he would have expected, the Honourable Pat Considine. It was four o'clock in the afternoon, but that gentleman already showed signs of having had recourse to artificial means for driving away dull care. Perhaps that accounted for the visit, and his being apparently oblivious of the fact that Cecil had cut him for the last half dozen years.

"Hullo, old chap, thought I'd look in and see how you are getting along on it all. What a blanked sell it was, wasn't it?" said Pat, swaying backwards and forwards, as he leant against a chest of drawers.

"How the devil did you find me out? What do you want here?" asked Cecil, who felt that Pat's having the impudence to call on him, was very ominous of his impending disgrace.

"I've been looking up old Freddy Seedyman, who lives at the top of the house, and I thought I'd drop in as I passed your door and chirp you up a bit," said Pat, and he stared at Cecil unsteadily for a minute or so, unembarrassed by his silence, and by the obvious fact that he was not grateful for being visited in his sickness.

Cecil was thinking out a bitterly sarcastic speech, when Pat broke the silence :

"I say, old chap, they're talking a deal about you to-day," he said, grinning maliciously.

"Who are, your lot?"

"All lots—every one who goes racing, and a good many who don't. They all have a bit to say about you, and some of 'em mix me up in it, which they have no right to do; for you kept me out of it, but I won't grumble about that now, it's just as well as it is."

"What lies are they saying about me?"

"Why, that you were standing in with Beamish and Kit Lukes, and were going to stop the Crier. That now the horse has won, you can't settle your bets. It's old Beamie's fault. You see the Crier just broke him, and after the race he began to curse your name before every one, and said it was all your infernal obstinacy for riding in the first race. He set a lot of talk going round. So now they are saying nasty things of you at the clubs; so Freddy Seedyman, who still belongs to the 'Rag' and the 'Turf,' says. You see, they are dead against Kit Lukes and Beamish. That's why they're all so awfully down on me. They're as bad themselves, half of 'em, and would do anything, but they won't stand Kit and Beamie, or any one who is in with them."

"It's a lie, and I believe it is only you, and fellows like you, who say it. Let me tell you, Mr. Pat, that whatever they say about me, I don't want the honour of your acquaintance, which I dispensed with half a dozen years ago."

"Nobody asked you, my boy. We draw the line at being warned off the turf, and there are plenty without you," said Pat.

"A gentleman wishes to see you—Mr.

Lukes. I told him you weren't able to see any one, but he said you would see him," said a servant.

"Kit Lukes will be about as pleasant to meet as a bear with a sore head, as I dare say you will find out. I'm off," said Pat. In a few seconds Mr. Lukes entered. To do him justice he seemed to bear his losses well. He looked as fresh and prosperous as ever. A slight puffiness under the eyes, told, perhaps, of the life he had led since he saw the Crier's number go up, but there were no other signs in his sleek, fresh-complexioned face. He was as scrupulously dressed as ever, in a cut-away Melton coat, a thick buff waistcoat, and a wonderfully well cut pair of pepper-and-salt trousers. He seemed, for him, to be in an unusually good temper.

" So Pat has been here ?" he said, after he had inquired about Cecil's health.

" Yes, confound his impudence. He is the last man I want to have in my rooms," answered Cecil savagely.

" And you didn't want him to see me here ; don't be afraid. He talks a lot, does the Honourable Pat Considine, but drunk or sober, he doesn't talk of what I tell him to keep to himself."

" It would be well, if another of your friends had kept a little more guard on his tongue; from what that fellow has told me, it seems that Beamish has been talking about me publicly," retorted Cecil, "he's an infernal savage, not fit to be trusted in civilized society."

"Well, he and I are two, now; but never mind what he said. You have only got to settle your account, and hold your head up, and all the talk in the world won't hurt you."

"Pay up! It's all very fine to talk like that, but how the devil am I to pay up? You don't suppose I can do that. Hang it all, do you think if I had any money, I should have gone in with you?" and Cecil laughed bitterly.

"It's a very awkward affair, if you can't settle, and it will cause a very unpleasant exposure. I have lost more than I can afford, as it is. Now I'm not going to throw it in your teeth, that you brought about this loss. That is past and gone, but I can't afford to be let in by you. Beamish seemed to think I paid for the three, but I don't lose much by him, for I took care to save myself, by getting everything he had as security. Now, you owe me six thousand pounds," said Mr. Lukes, and he looked grimly at a betting-book.

"You have everything I have in the

world. A lien on the money I get on leaving the service, and a cheque for all the ready money I have, which no doubt you have used by this time."

"You are right; and that leaves you over four thousand to the bad. Now, I must have that four thousand, Captain Warleigh."

"Don't talk rot! It's not as if it were all I owed. There's twelve hundred I laid Dargle, and six hundred to Burke of the regiment. I can't pay them, so it's no good my worrying my head about you. The talk has begun, and it can go on. As soon as I am well enough to get away I leave England for good and all. To-day I send in my papers. It's all up with me, and as for getting anything out of me— You may whistle for it," said Cecil, taking a cigarette and lighting it.

Kit Lukes did not show any signs of being discontented. He stared at his betting-book and seemed to work out figures.

"What you want is about eight thousand pounds, and then you could settle and laugh at all the infernal chatter of these swells, nine-tenths of whom are defaulters themselves."

"Well, I have not got it, and don't see my way to getting it, so I must try and laugh without settling," said Cecil coolly.

Still Mr. Lukes was not irritated.

" It's a pity, Captain. You won't like the life you'll have to lead. · You are not like Pat Considine now, who would sooner hang about the West End bars, and pal up with sharpers and scoundrels, than frequent decent society. He is happier in bringing off some twopenny-halfpenny robbery in a low billiard-room, than he would be in a club with his brother and his brother's pals. But you are cut out for the swells, Captain ; and you'll never get along with the sweeps."

" I don't intend to try. I wish I had never known any of them," answered Cecil, with a look that pointed the insult of his words.

" Eight thousand pounds. Couldn't you manage to raise it ? It isn't so very much. Haven't you any reversions or anything ? A man like you—old family and all that sort of thing—and have to go to the bad, just for eight thousand pounds."

Cecil didn't take the trouble to reply, but intimated by a shake of the head that he hadn't a penny.

" Supposing I were to manage to get it for you. Ay ! what would you say to that ? You would pay a pretty stiff price for the money, and wouldn't talk about percentage, when it came to signing a bill or bond," said Mr. Lukes, and he pushed his hands deep down into his pockets, and stared straight into Cecil's face.

"*Get it for me!* What do you want me to do for it?" Cecil answered. He knew enough of Mr. Lukes to be sure that he had some scheme in his head, and looking into his face he noticed an expression there that startled him; and then, all at once, an idea came into his mind that made his heart jump with hope, and he said,—

"By George! There's nothing wrong with Jack, my nephew, is there? He has not broken his neck out hunting or anything of that sort?"

"Don't be agitated, you have no cause for anxiety. As far as I know, Sir John is as fit and well as he was last Friday at Liverpool. But let us cut matters short. Will you give me a bill for fifty thousand pounds, if I get you eight thousand?"

"*Fifty thousand pounds!* If my bond is worth anything, it is worth more than eight thousand, and I can get more than that for it."

"Can you? Go and see; go round to the Jews and Christians who deal in

money, and find out how many of 'em
will even take the trouble to see you. I
am throwing good money after bad.
But, as it is a question of losing three
thousand by you anyhow, or trying to
pull you through, I might risk it."

"What do you want? My bond for
fifty thousand? No, you have something
else in your head. You know something,
and until I know what that is, I will sign
nothing."

Mr. Lukes smiled pleasantly, brushed
his glossy silk hat, and put his betting
book into his pocket.

"As you like, Captain, only it's a pity.
You won't get the money elsewhere.
The little talk there is now, will become
a good deal worse when Lord Dargle and
Major Burke find that they can't get
their money, and it is known that you
commissioned me to lay against the Crier,
and back Blue Ruin to the tune of six
thousand. It will only end in your signing anything I like for as many hundreds
as I offer thousands. I daresay you think
you're right, Captain; but remember this:
if I do know anything, no one else does,
and no one else will advance you eight
thousand pounds, or one-tenth of it."

"What on earth could the fellow
know? Cecil thought, and he wondered

from what possible source any increase of
fortune could have come to him.

"To-morrow will suit me as well as to-
day, and next week as well as this, only
may-be it won't be quite.,the same to
you. Send Lord Dargle and Major Burke
cheques to-day—they are both in town—
and by sending a *commissionaire* they would
have their cheques in half-an-hour, and
all talk there is about you would be
stopped. In another week, things will
look uglier. All I ask is your bond for
fifty thousand. Why, when I think of
how any one else would treat such a document, I am amazed at my moderation."

"But you know something. You
would never part with a penny unless
you knew something," said Cecil, "something is wrong with Jack."

"I should say the odds in favour of
Sir John surviving you would be about
four to one. Then it's odds against his
dying without a son. An insurance office
would tell you what your chances of
coming into his estates are worth. You
can't raise the money from any one else ;
and if you try to do so, you'll have to
pay me every penny, or I'll break you.
But take your time to think over it. I
can wait, if you can," and Mr. Lukes
moved a pace or two towards the door.

" Yes, Lukes could wait," Cecil thought, "but it was a very different matter with him."

After all, if the lawyer liked to speculate in the remote chances of his succeeding his nephew, why should he baulk him? It was possible that he thought it would pay him to throw a little good money after bad, so as to keep a debtor going. He hated the fellow, and felt that he was always to be in his power. But to get the money on any terms, was more than he expected. He would be out of his troubles for the present, and men's mouths would be shut.

"Well, what do you say?" asked Lukes, who read his decision in his face. "You'll do it. Well, you are wise," and as Cecil growled out his consent, the lawyer rang the bell.

"I want a couple of witnesses for a document, and a *commissionaire* to take the letters to Dargle and Burke, and my cheque to the bank," he answered to Cecil's question, as to what he wanted.

CHAPTER III.

LIMBS OF THE LAW.

"WELL," said Lukes, after the bond had been duly signed and witnessed, and the two witnesses had left the room, "that document may be more valuable than you think. I have a bit of news to tell you. You have, may-be, a right this minute, to call yourself Sir Cecil Warleigh."

"You have done me, Jack's dead," said Cecil savagely.

"You are an affectionate uncle," sneered Lukes, "and yet they say he was very good to you. But don't be afraid. He is well enough, only, whether he is Sir John Warleigh or no, is another thing."

Cecil stared at the lawyer incredulously. Here was one of the sharpest men he knew, and he had got hold of some absurd notion that his brother's son was not the heir to the baronetcy and estates. Anyhow, he had got the money from Lukes, that was a comfort. It would be too late in the day for the lawyer to cry off when he found out that he had discovered a mare's nest.

"Oh, you are not certain that he is Sir John. Who do you suppose is the baronet?" he asked.

"Who should be, with your nephew out of the running? Why, you of course."

"Oh, I am, am I? I was under the impression that the law of primogeniture settled these things, and that my elder brother's son would cut me out. Are you sure I am not a duke or a marquis? for if you can upset Jack, then you can upset pretty nearly any one else."

"The eldest son's son cuts out the second son as you say, only he must happen to be legitimate, and Sir John Warleigh labours under the disadvantage of having been born out of wedlock."

"Well, if you can prove that, I come in all right; only, as I can remember about the wedding—though I was but a youngster at the time—and as my brother married the daughter of a parson at Fetchester, whom every one in that town knows, I don't think Jack would ever have much trouble in proving his legitimacy."

"Captain John Warleigh happened at

the time of the wedding to be a married man, with a wife living."

"I don't believe it. He wouldn't have done such a thing," said Cecil, thinking of Helen Warleigh's sad, beautiful face, and remembering the character his brother had always borne of being honourable and good-hearted, though he had been reckless and extravagant enough.

"Dare say he wouldn't, only you see he did. Listen to this," said Lukes, and then clearly enough, he related all the facts he had learned from Sam Paradine, and afterwards tested; and beside that, another fact. He had found out the house where Captain and Mrs. Warleigh lived after the marriage at Brighton, and had got hold of the landlady, who would give evidence. The handwriting in the register had been examined and compared, and the expert swore that it was the same as some undoubted signature of the alleged bridegroom. Altogether the case appeared to be a very strong one.

"But the motive. What earthly motive could he have had in doing such an infernally blackguard thing?" asked Cecil, who was still inclined to be sceptical.

"Motive! Why, I suppose he took a fancy to the girl, and then got sick of her ; or he might have thought she was dead, or he might have had a hundred different motives. It is the counsel who is defending that is always talking about motive, and he generally makes out that the prisoner never could have had any earthly reason for doing what he has been clearly proved to have done. But show me what a fellow did, and hanged if I care why he did it ; and that Captain John Warleigh, your half-brother, committed bigamy the day he went through the ceremony of marriage with Helen, daughter of the Reverend Dalton, Vicar of St. Paul's Fetchester, I am pretty certain I can prove in a court of law. The cheque I have given you shows that, I should guess. And now take my advice, and go and put your case in a lawyer's hands.

" You are a lawyer, aren't you ? " said Cecil, who began to believe in his chances, and thought no one could understand the case better than the man who had got it up.

" Yes, I am a lawyer, but it's an uncharitable world, and, between you and me, there are a good many people who would not think any better of your case because Kit Lukes was your attorney. The more disreputable your case is, the more respectable your lawyer should be, for there ain't much chance of getting hold of one who will find it too shady for him to touch, if there is much to be made out of it. Not that our case is at all shady, only the prejudice will be against us. You see, your nephew is popular. Cohen is your man, Augustus Cohen, he is sharp, eminently respectable, the judges have got into a way of complimenting him on his high professional honour and that sort of thing and, at the same time, he is a man of the world, and I can get on with him."

If Cohen, whom every one knew about, believed in the case, then things would indeed look favourable, thought Cecil, and after all Kit Lukes generally knew what he was doing, and when it came to his being willing to risk a large sum of money on his proving a right to the title and estates, it looked as if he thought very highly of his chances. It was true that Lukes was practically taking something like twenty-four to one, as he risked two thousand pounds to win fifty thousand; but the outsider that Kit Lukes backed at twenty to one, generally had a six to four chance.

"Yes, let us go and see Cohen. I can get about somehow," said Cecil, eager to get the best possible opinion about his case.

"No, Captain Warleigh, take care of yourself, remember your life is worth a pot of money now. Keep still, where you are, and we will get Cohen to come here. I'll write to him, I know him well enough; he was against me in one or two little businesses I was mixed up in, and he said some very nasty things about me in the police court. Jews always seem to think that none but their own people have any right to be a little clever. However, Cohen and I understand each other, when we are by ourselves."

"When would Cohen come? How long would he want to think over the case before he gave an opinion? When would the case come on in court?" and a good many other questions were asked by Cecil, who began to look flushed and triumphant.

Kit Lukes promised to go at once to Cohen's office—which was situated in the shadow of Newgate prison—and make an appointment with him.

"I daresay he will come in here on his way to the office. You'll find him pleasant enough, particularly if he believes you are going to be a baronet—he goes in for being the trusted friend of the British aristocracy; and as he began life as the thieves' friend, getting up *alibis* and defending pickpockets and mags-men, he thinks he has made a big rise in the world. It's just like those Jews. They can do any amount of dirty work, and none of the dirt seem to stick to 'em."

Cecil Warleigh felt amused as he heard Lukes snarling at the great criminal lawyer, for his memory went back to a notorious turf-swindle that had been exposed in a police court, and to Cohen's scathing cross-examination of Lukes, whose character was never completely blackened until that day.

"How you hate him! I suppose you never will forgive him," said Cecil, laughing pleasantly.

"*Hate* him! No, I don't any more than I do the jockey who just does me on the post. Why should you hate a man you can hire? No, I tell you, Cohen and 1 are very good friends when no one is looking on."

That evening Cecil got a telegram from Lukes, saying that Mr. Cohen would call in the morning, and about ten o'clock the two lawyers met in his rooms.

Mr. Cohen was a good-looking little man with a good deal of manner. Some people would call him a very gentlemanly man, though no one would mistake him for a gentleman in the true sense of the word. His slight figure was well, but rather too smartly dressed. There was an indescribable something about him in the movement of his neck, and in the glitter of his eyes, which reminded one of a ferret or a weasel.

Cecil had some slight acquaintance with Mr. Cohen, for he was a man who went a good deal into society. Early in his life he had learnt the advantage of such indirect advertising as etiquette allows a professional man. He had plenty of acquaintances on the press, and newspaper-readers soon became very familiar with his characteristics as a cross-examiner and a police court advocate. Again and again had clever descriptive reporters made copy out of him, his gentlemanly manners and other attributes, real or imaginary. The class of practice he laid himself out for was immensely helped by advertisement, and he prospered. The pickpocket and the burglar soon found that they could no longer command his services, and the aristocratic delinquent, and the merchant-prince, who had overstepped the thin fence that separated clever trading from crime, found him a great help in trouble. It is characteristic of the age which so devoutly worships celebrity of almost any sort, that he managed to get into society which a few years ago no solicitor could have entered, much less one who was at the call of Bill Sykes and company. Still, wherever he went he was at ease, and perfectly pleased with himself and his position.

" You would be surprised, if I told you all I know about people who are here," he would say when he met an old acquaintance at some brilliant gathering of the fashionable world. To do him justice, he never did tell what he knew, and was perfectly loyal to his clients. And he did know a great deal, and had been consulted in many a delicate affair which never became public.

" Every stone in that house is a compounded felony," snarled one disagreeable critic, on passing the splendid mansion Mr. Augustus Cohen had built for himself across the park. Possibly he had never done anything which the law could characterize so harshly, but he had hushed many an awkward scandal, which might, had it not been for him, have grown into a criminal prosecution.

Besides the criminal practice in which he especially excelled, his services were in great request in civil actions, when

knowledge of human nature, particularly
of its worst side, was the one thing most
needful in the lawyer employed.   He
prided himself in never being deceived in
his own client, and he seldom or never
took up a civil case unless the chances
were in favour of his winning it.

Cecil, as he lay back on a sofa, smoking
a cigarette, watched, with an amused
interest, the demeanour of the two
lawyers towards each other.   They appeared, however, to have forgotten all
about their mutual police-court experiences.

Mr. Lukes was not one whit em-
barrassed, and the two evidently understood each other.

"Mr. Lukes had better tell you the
facts of the case, he knows them, and can
explain them pretty clearly," Cecil began.

" I am sure no one can explain them
more clearly than our friend Lukes will.
It is a pity he does not devote more
time to the practice of the profession he
honours ; but, as it is, the law's loss is the
turf's gain," said Mr. Cohen.

" It isn't your fault that I devote any
of my time to it," answered Kit, refer-
ring to the occasion when Cohen's cross-
examination had nearly caused him to be
struck off the roll.   " However, you don't

want to hear me talk about myself—the
facts are pretty simple." And he put the
matter before Cohen.

" How did you get to know about
this ? " asked Cohen, turning round his
head in his police-court manner, and
taking a quick look into Luke's face.

Cecil had never thought of asking this
question, but it seemed to him to be very
apposite, in regard to whether or no the
whole case was fraudulently concocted.
Lukes, however, answered it easily
enough, and told how Sam Paradine had
found it all out in course of his search for
the children of John Matterson.

Mr. Cohen made an entry in his note-
book, and appeared, so far, to be satisfied. It would be easy to satisfy himself
as to the existence of a fund in which
some one of the name of Matterson was
interested. This point, though nothing
to do with the case directly, seemed to him
to be of considerable importance, as tend-
ing to prove the *bonâ fides* of the case set
up on behalf of Cecil.

" The evidence of identification is the
main point. Was it really Captain John
Warleigh, who married Sarah Matterson ?
Let's see, what does that amount to ?
There's Mrs. Butlin—she says that she
had seen Captain Warleigh, in uniform, on

two occasions, with the regiment; then
there is Butlin, the landlord, he says that
he saw Captain Warleigh on three or four
occasions, at races and cricket matches,
and that he was the same man who
afterwards frequented his house and
married Sarah Matterson."

" That evidence may be a little slight;
but there is the matter of the cheque,
which I maintain clenches it," answered
Lukes.

" Does it, do you think? I am doubtful if you would like that view, if you had
my experience ; but it is just the sort of
point a jury would catch at, and I think
you have a strongish case, if your witnesses will support it, and the other side
haven't any answer to it.

" What answer to it can they have? "
asked Lukes with a triumphant smile.

" That remains to be proved, but I will
look into matters, and in a few days we
may begin proceedings," said Cohen,
" by writing to claim the estates. I
suppose there will be no question of a
compromise ? "

" No, my nephew might give up without a fight, if he thought we were in the
right, though that is not likely, for it
would entail his admitting that his father
was a scoundrel, and that his mother was

not legally married, and that he would
never believe. No, he never would compromise. It is unpleasant, causing so much
family scandal ; but it can't be helped."

"That is not your fault, Captain Warleigh. Believe me, I have hushed up as
many awkward stories as most men. I
can assure you, that, if it were reported
that I had got light-headed, and was
beginning to tell all I knew, a good
many very distinguished persons would
feel most uncomfortable ; but I have never
seen a secret hushed up that affected the
ownership of property. Family honour
is all very well, but it is not priceless."

" I am sorry for my nephew ; but no one
can expect me to forego my just rights,
and I must say that I have not found
him particularly considerate to me," said
Cecil, at the same time wondering what
view the world would take of his conduct,
and determining that he would hold his
own, and defy hostile opinion.

Mr. Cohen smiled acquiescence, as he
shook hands cordially with Cecil, and took
a colder farewell of Mr. Lukes.

" Ah, he believes we are going to win,
and he is a very clever little chap, though
he is always posing and attitudinizing to
the penny-a-liners," said Mr. Lukes, when
the lawyer had gone.

CHAPTER IV.

JACK WARLEIGH IS DISTURBED AND CONSOLED.

SOME days after the interview at Cecil Warleigh's chambers, a hansom stopped at No. — New Square, Lincoln's Inn, out of which Jack Warleigh jumped, and ascended the stairs leading to the office of Mr. Grimshaw, three steps at a time. There was a sense of hurry about him that unfavourably impressed the old clerk who opened the door. Haste was a quality thoroughly out of keeping with the office. Clients who were in a hurry were put to cool in a dusty room with a window looking on to a dead wall. The walls of this room were covered with dusty volumes of Law Reports that might have been dummies, for they were never taken down and read. There was an office table with the supplement of a *Times* two months old, some ancient numbers of a legal newspaper, an inkpot full of curiously crusted ink, a pen-stand, and a pen-holder without a pen.

Jack Warleigh was not the only man who had fidgeted about in that room. Many a client had spent a bad quarter of an hour in that dreary apartment, fraught with a gloomy tale of dipped estates, importunate creditors, and agricultural depression. Advice had been sought there by, many a country client, as to what could be done, when it was already too late to do anything to save his estates.

After Jack had paced the room, again and again, taken up some of the dusty newspapers, thrown them down, read the names of the "Reports," wondered what they were about, and breathed a wish uncomplimentary to the law and lawyers, at last Mr. Grimshaw came in, apologizing for keeping him waiting, and asking him into his own office, where, surrounded by his beloved tin-boxes, he sat and wrote hundreds of letters.

"I have come about this thing. I can't understand what on earth it means," said Jack, as he gave the lawyer a letter.

Mr. Grimshaw leisurely put on a pair of gold-rimmed spectacles and began to read.

"Hum! 'Mr. Augustus Cohen—' I have no doubt a very respectable person in his own line in the profession ; a name

one constantly meets with in the papers—
' Mr. Augustus Cohen, Solicitor, of Newgate Street,' said he, as he began the letter,
which took him some time to read, " this
is, Sir John, I may say a letter—a
lawyer's letter—practically demanding on
behalf of his client, Captain Cecil Warleigh,
the Warleigh Estates, and the baronetcy
—and then he goes into the question of a
marriage between your late father and
one Sarah Matterson, stating further, that
Sarah Matterson was alive when your
father married again. He states also, that
he has personally convinced himself of the
bonâ fides of the claim, and hopes that
something may be done to prevent the
scandal of a trial, which would make public
property of the unfortunate conduct of
your father, and the unhappy circumstances surrounding the second marriage
ceremony he went through."

" That is how he talks of my mother's
marriage," said Jack.

" Yes, yes ; certainly, Mr. Augustus
Cohen is, I believe, a very useful person
in his own line, but I think it really
perhaps would be better taste if he would
not mix himself up in a matter of this
nature, involving a claim to an old family
title and property. Personally we never
do care for litigious business, and Mr.

Augustus Cohen is not quite in our line,
but in your case Sir John, we shall be
proud to act, and we will write to this
gentleman."

"But what is the meaning of the
letter? Surely Cecil has never told this
fellow to make a demand of this sort.
Don't you see that this infernal statement
about two marriages dishonours my father
and my mother?"

"This claim is very unlikely to have
been made without Captain Cecil Warleigh's concurrence. Captain Warleigh
is a gentleman of very expensive tastes,
and somewhat limited means, and probably the family disgrace would be borne
much more easily by him than his own
bankruptcy, which I have always considered an impending event. In fact,
you may set your mind at rest about that,
for Mr Cohen is respectable—thoroughly
respectable, and would never have written
this without Captain Warleigh's concurrence."

"But don't you see the shame of this
charge against my father—the utter
impossibility of his having acted such a
cruel, cowardly, and treacherous part?"

"Yes, certainly, certainly, that is a
very proper view to take of the matter—
a very proper one, indeed. I take it, Sir

John, you never personally knew your father?" asked Mr. Grimshaw, "you remind me of him in many respects."

The old lawyer did not share Jack's confidence, he could remember John Warleigh the elder, as the wild cavalry officer whose name was always in men's mouths for some act of reckless extravagance,—of daring,—or mad escapade, and had spent the fortune his mother had left him, in a few months.

"That Cecil Warleigh should try to bring this dishonour upon us all, was more than I could believe when I read the letter—but since you say he has done this, I suppose I must believe it.—You, then, will answer this letter, and say that it is an impudent attempt at extortion."

"Well, I don't know about attempt at extortion. Mr. Cohen is quite a respectable man, though I do feel, when one is concerned against him, that the old professional lines and landmarks are being done away with. But we will defend the case and look into this matter. By the way, perhaps some of your father's old friends might know something about it; if you were to ask them where he was, and what he was doing about this time."

"I don't like to let any of them know that such a disgraceful charge has been made by one of our family—disgraceful to the man who makes it, I mean," said Jack, boldly enough.

He had not troubled himself much about the loss of fortune and title; all he cared for was the slight that had been put on his father and mother, and the dirty trick that Cecil had tried to play him.

Old Grimshaw, however, by no means took so light a view of the matter. The elder John Warleigh was not a person for whose memory the old lawyer had much respect. The best thing he had ever done was getting killed at Balaklava. That he should have made a low marriage, was, after all, only what one or two noble clients of his—whose names he could see on their tin boxes—had done. Certainly, that he should afterwards have committed bigamy was rather a strong measure; but then, there is no telling what a man like Captain John Warleigh might not do.

To Mr. Grimshaw, who was a good while married, the notion of any one committing bigamy was monstrously unreasonable.

Jack walked away from the lawyer's, without having gained much comfort.

The second person he talked about the matter to was General Cottingham, whom he met in Pall Mall.

"Nonsense, my lad, don't trouble your-

self about it. Your father was—well, I
suppose it won't hurt you to hear about
it—as wild as a hawk, but he was as
honourable a man as ever breathed. I
don't believe this story. Nothing could
ever make me," said the General. "I
can remember his talking to me the day
before he was killed. We had a notion
that the cavalry would not be kept idle
much longer, and he had a presentiment
—that his saddle would be emptied—as
many another fellow had, who came
home safe and sound—and that night he
talked about his marriage—and how
happy it had made him—and his youth
and the money he had wasted—and the
follies he had been guilty of. He had
been foolish, wickedly foolish, but hadn't
ever wronged any man or woman. You
know how men will talk at such times.
No, you'll never get me to believe he had
any crime on his mind."

"Thanks, General, I was not afraid
that you would ever have believed it, but
that Cecil should have been at the bottom
of this—that cuts me up."

"It isn't quite the right thing, but
poor old Cecil has a lot of temptations,
you know, and somehow or other, he is a
little less able to fight against them than
other fellows seem to be. I always liked

him from the day he joined the regiment,
but I noticed that about him," said the
General, rather to himself than to Jack,
hardly remembering that he was not giving his friend a very good character.

" But he must have known it was an
infernal lying story against his own half-
brother."

" Known it—I don't suppose he remembers much about your father, and I
don't think that Cecil does believe much
in his fellow-men. While as for being
his own—I don't suppose he thinks his
own family better than other people's.
Why should he? the member of it whom,
I suppose, he knows best, namely himself,
isn't so very strait-laced. What do the
lawyers say about this? Have you seen
any of them?"

" Old Grimshaw seems to think it
serious, at least he treats it seriously."

" Quite right too, it's their business to
treat things seriously, one doesn't go to
them to hear them make jokes. But set
your mind at rest, it's all nonsense. Jack
Warleigh might have thrown himself away
for a pretty face, but he never would have
married your mother if he had another
wife. Pooh! nonsense. I'll tell Cecil that
he is in the wrong box, and that some one is
persuading him to play a very poor part."

"Are you going home? because I will come with you. I would like to talk to Kate about this."

"Come along, my boy," said the General, "but I should not make too much of it to Kate, you know, women do not understand these things."

"I think she ought to know, though it is not a nice subject to talk to her about," answered Jack, looking grave enough.

Cottingham looked rather grave too. An uneasy feeling came into his mind, that perhaps Jack would hardly find Kate as sympathetic as he expected. She had no undue amount of sentiment in her, and most likely on hearing Jack's story, it would occur to her to think how, if Cecil's claims were well-founded, it would affect her prospects.

He was a good young fellow was Jack Warleigh, only he had yet to go through the somewhat painful process of learning what men and women were like.

"By-the-bye, what was the date of this pretended marriage at Brighton?" the General asked, half in order to turn his thoughts from a subject which was worrying him.

"March," answered Jack.

"Wonder where I was then? That's the worst of growing old—one remembers some things as if they were yesterday,

like that talk I had with poor old Jack at
Balaklava—but there are stretches of
time about which one remembers nothing. If we could only prove where he
was on that day, there would be an end
of it; but I suppose the cock-and-bull
story will tumble to pieces as soon as it
is properly looked into," said the General.
And as they walked on to Kensington,
he chatted on pleasantly enough about
different subjects, and pretended to think
very little about the lawyer's letter. For
all that, he felt gloomy; Cecil had gone
wrong, so it seemed to him. Those
stories that men told after the Grand
National had reached his ears, and he
had not at all liked them.

"Confounded nuisance, that all the
people one liked would do such infernally
crooked things," thought the General.
Then he was not quite certain in his own
mind that Cecil might not succeed. He
had no exaggerated faith in virtue always
being triumphant, and he believed that to
have Mr. Augustus Cohen on one's side,
in legal proceedings, was better than to
have a good conscience.

When Jack Warleigh got to the
General's house, he told his trouble to
Kate. He saw no shade of vexation or
trouble in her calm pale face. There was
a tone of sympathy in her voice, when she

expressed her surprise that Cecil had
played so mean a part.

" But, if this is proved true, would it
not make you feel different towards me ? "
said Jack.

" Different ! No, how should it ? You
would always be the same to me," she
answered, and a soft light seemed to come
into her grey eyes in answer to the look of
joy that her words brought into Jack's face.

" Poor boy," she thought, " why should
he not be happy while it was possible ?
Sufficient for the day is the evil thereof ;
and there would be plenty of time for him
to learn how little he really was to her."

" It's a confounded shame, if Kate's
fooling him," the General thought, as he
watched her with Jack. " How like she
is to her mother ! " Guy Cottingham's
married life had been a short one, but it
had been long enough for him to shudder
at this thought ; either Kate cared a
good deal less for her future husband's
loss of property and title than he believed
she did, or she was making a fool of Jack
Warleigh. Well, some men seemed born to
be made fools of by women. Jack Warleigh
was one of them. Only for the time being,
it seemed to make him happy. So the
General argued to himself, stroked his
moustache, and tried to look on the bright
side of things. After all, there was

nothing, most likely, in Cecil's claim, and
Jack would never, perhaps, find Kate out.

If Jack Warleigh had been present at
an interview in Kensington Gardens the
morning before, he would have understood how it was that she took the news
he had brought to her with such unruffled
calm. He would have heard Cecil, as
they paced the flower walk, unheeded by
the swarm of nursery maids and children.
give Kate a very concise summary of Mr.
Augustus Cohen's opinion of his chances
of ousting his nephew.

"Don't look at me like that, Cecil. I am
sure you are reminding the nursery-maid.
who is staring at us, of the last chapter
she read in a penny novel."

"Well, what I say is, I would like to
wait and see how things go," she had
said, after she had heard it all, and Cecil
had begun to talk—as she said—foolishly.
"No, it's no earthly use going into heroics.
I dare say I am cold-blooded. I should
be a great deal more comfortable with
you than with Jack. Anyone so terribly
and horridly green as he is becomes very
wearying and heavy in hand, after a
little—but all your plans go askew so.
You are always just beaten on the post.
There was the fortune you would have
made on the horse that ran second at
Liverpool, if only you had ridden the one

that came in first, but even that went all wrong."

"It won't go all wrong this time. If you marry Jack—you marry a man without a name or a penny."

"You may be perfectly certain I shall do no such thing until this is disposed of one way or the other, but in the meantime there is no good in making the poor boy wretched about it. If he loses his estates he loses me too; but he'll bear his trouble best by taking it at a gulp—all at once," Kate had said; and then she had parted with Cecil, and gone back to her father's house, thinking calmly over the news she had heard. A young curate, who passed her, looked into her soft sweet face, and thought that the look of rest in it was extremely Madonna-like.

So, when Jack told her his story, she did not show any anxiety—which perhaps she might have been excused in doing—for such important things as money and position. She professed not to believe the story.

"And there is something that you won't lose, whatever the lawyers take from you," she whispered to him, as he went away. Perhaps, after all, the General was right—certainly, for the 'time being,' Jack was happy.

CHAPTER V.

"THE OLD LARK PIE."

WHILE Kit Lukes and Cecil Warleigh
were finding plenty to console them for
the result of the great steeple-chase, that
bold outlaw Colonel Beamish found himself compelled to go under. Mr. Lukes
had taken care to provide himself against
the contingency of the Colonel's not
caring to pay his share of the losses,
should any unforeseen misfortune upset
this carefully devised plot. The Colonel's
capital consisted almost entirely of
steeple-chasers and racers in training, in
most of which Lukes already had a half-
share, and he took care to hold the
Colonel's half as security for the heavy
bets he had laid for him. That there
was no getting that property back from
Kit the Colonel fully realized.

Other than his horses, the Colonel had
little else than a couple of hundred
pounds. On the other hand, he had

made, on his own responsibility, bets to the amount of about eight hundred pounds. That money he never for one moment thought of paying. To sacrifice all his capital to paying one-half his debts was an act of folly he was not in the slightest degree tempted to commit. Kit Lukes would not help him. Their partnership, the lawyer had pointed out, was at an end, and now Beamish had no share in what had been the partnership property.

"No, Colonel Beamish, as you choose to call yourself, I will listen to none of your insolence. I have had enough of it already, and now you are a broken defaulter, who can be of no use to any one, it is not likely I shall submit to any more. If you molest or talk to me, you will find yourself inside a police court," was Mr. Lukes' final remark to him at the interview on the day after the race for the Grand National.

After all he did not see that he had any definite grievance against the lawyer. He certainly had no hold on him. For to spread the report of his having been mixed up with him in an abortive attempt to have the Crier pulled would not do Lukes much mischief. It might damage his character for shrewdness, but

would leave his reputation for honesty
pretty much where it was before.

So the Colonel accepted the situation.
His career as an owner of race-horses, and
a swell—as he put it—was over. He had
come out of it, too, with the two hundred
pounds in his pocket, and he fancied he
could find something better to do with
that than paying his debts.

After some consideration as to the
desirability or otherwise of paying his
bill, and having decided that honesty,
to that extent, was the best policy, he
removed from Tankard's Hotel. Constantly meeting people one owes money
to is bad for all parties, and entails a
needless waste of nerve tissue. To disappear, for all practical purposes, in
London, does not entail any very long
journey. The other side of Leicester
Square was quite far enough for the
Colonel's purposes. A little tavern
situated at the end of a court gave him
the modest accommodation and the quiet
which he wanted.

"Well, I never, if it ain't Colonel
Beamish. Why, we 'aven't seen you for
this ever so long, hardly since you came
back to England. You've been so grand,
owning race-horses and what not, that we
thought you'd forgotten all about us,"

said the landlady, who jumped up from
her chair behind the bar when she saw
Beamish, and shook hands with him with
great cordiality.

"Is the room I used to have five years
ago unoccupied?" Beamish asked, after
he had been served with some refreshment.

"Yes, it is, since Captain Chalker got
into that trouble six weeks ago. But
surely that little room won't be quite good
enough for a rich man like you are now,
Colonel?"

"Oh, quite good enough for me, missus,
I hope I shall never come to anything
worse, and between you and me, I ain't
so very rich."

"Why, I heard you were in rare luck,"
said the landlady, "the parties you knew,
as used to come here, used to be always
talking about you and your luck."

"I'll be bound to say, though, you have
heard them say a deal about me and my
bad luck during the last day or two.
Yes, my good luck has come to an
end for the present. I can't complain, I
had a pretty good slice of it. It began at
Lima, four years ago, when I found myself one morning walking home with my
pockets crammed with notes after having
broken the bank at a gambling place
there. I was thinking that all the notes

would sooner or later find their way back
where they came from, when I saw a
vessel that was bound for home just
getting up her steam in the harbour.
The thought came over me all at once
that they should never get a dollar of
their money back, and I ran as hard as I
could set legs to the ground, to the quay,
and jumped on board the ship just as she
was beginning to move. There I was
with no berth taken, no luggage, nothing
but a suit of white clothes, the pockets of
which were crammed with paper money.
All I thought of was that I'd be off home
and take my dollars with me, and from
that out, I did fairly well, until the other
day, when I got broke over the Liverpool
Grand National."

"Which I am sure I am sorry for,
Colonel, whatever others may be, and
you're welcome back here again. You'll
find a goodish few you used to know use
the room still. Some dead—and there—
one or two like Captain Chalker in trouble.
It was having a cheque-book as caused
all the unpleasantness as ended in his
getting one year's 'hard.' It's a sad
pity to think of the trouble as cheque-
books does cause gentlemen to get into,
when they keeps 'em after they are done
with having banking accounts."

" Who are alive, then, and out of gaol ? "
asked Beamish.

" Well, there's Nobby Tyler, and Tappie
Tarleton, and Flash Brady, they all come
here very often ; there has been a little
unpleasantness now and then, Brady
will try to use the place for business purposes, bringing parties here, and wanting
to have a good game at cards with 'em,
or toss for sovereigns, which is against
the rules of the house, and always have
been. But, putting that on one side,
everything has gone on snug and comfortable, and the gents meet here, as they
always did, and talk over racing, and
betting, and business, and behave themselves as well as the customers of any
house in London."

" The Old Lark Pie," like a good many
other London public-houses, had a dis-
tinct character. It was the meeting place
for what had almost become a club of
gentlemen who lived by their wits. Some
of them practised in a high class and re-
fined manner the calling of *welcher* on
the turf. Others devoted themselves to
games nominally of chance, which, when
they played them, lost what the law con-
siders their objectionable character, for
they undoubtedly became games of skill.
Others were great at billiards. Some of

the elders used to talk of themselves as
capital skittle-players, and would lament
the decay of that fine old English game.
There was a pleasant sense of quiet about
"The Old Lark Pie." Those who frequented it were of the same profession, and
understood one another. They smoked
and drank there, untroubled by any
disturbing thought of business or money-
making ; for there was not the remotest
likelihood of any betting or gambling at
the "Pie," the frequenters knew each
other too well for that. It was a long
time since Beamish had sat and smoked
his pipe there, and yet he felt himself
thoroughly at home. During the last
year or two he had seen most of the frequenters of the place, but then the circumstance that he was an owner of race-
horses, and aspired to be a swell, as he
termed it, obliged him to keep clear of
them. He really looked forward to having
a good talk to some old friends. Some of
them might feel a little jealous of him,
for there was already a good deal too
much competition in their line, but no one
would show any resentment at his having
avoided them in his good times, for that
a member, when it suited his purpose to
do so, might cut the lot, was one of the
leges non scripta of the Society.

When the *habitués* of the house dropped
into the bar-parlour, one or two of them
recognized Beamish with considerable
cordiality.

"Glad to see you, Colonel. Now that
you have come back again to the old crib,
you'll agree that you might go further
and fare worse. The drink is good, the
place is quiet and cosy, and as for the
company 'one knows who one meets,'" said
one gentleman, and the Colonel expressed
his agreement with the sentiment. Sometimes one can hardly realize how time
passes ; and sitting in the bar-parlour of
' The Old Lark Pie,' with his pipe in his
mouth, listening to two gentlemen discussing the demerits of a certain seaside
race-meeting, he felt as if he had left it
only yesterday.

"A hawful trap of a place, that course
is, little better than a hiland, the sea on
two sides and a river on the third. Talk
about hexits from the the-a-tres, there
ought to be a hact of Parliament passed
against a course you can't slip away from
when a riotous mob wants to take the law
in their hown 'ands. Bless yer, I sees it
in my dreams, the sea all round an' a mob,
as savage as a tiger, a-running into me,"
one of the welchers was droning out, while
the other smoked and sympathized.

In the peaceful quiet of "The Old Lark Pie," welchers could recount the stirring episodes of their hazardous calling. The Three-card-man could explain the niceties and embellishments he had grafted on to his well-worn part, and the card and billiard sharper could explain the neat diplomacy of his art to appreciative listeners.

What is more pleasing than to be amongst yourselves, and to know whom you will meet? Beamish, as he sat and smoked, and drank the whisky of "The Pie," gracefully receiving the homage which was accorded to him as a party who had owned race-horses, was able to dream over his past glories, and to take his misfortune philosophically.

Sitting by himself in the back room one afternoon, he recognized a familiar voice outside in the bar, and heard the landlady mention a name he knew well enough.

"Why, Mr. Considine, you are a stranger, but I'm glad to see you looking well and hearty," she was saying.

"Hallo, Beamy my boy, who'd have thought of meeting you here? I went to Tankard's, and found that you had folded up your tent, 'like the Arabs, and as silently passed away.' From their man-

ner there, I fancied you had been a good
deal wanted since you left," said Pat, as
he went into the room.

"Didn't know this was a haunt of
yours," said Beamish, without showing
much enthusiasm at meeting the other.

"Nor is it. I drop in here now and
then, though. It's nice and quiet, and
just now I hardly know where to turn.
The bailiffs have got into my place down
in the country. The bookies are making
it warm about the little I owe 'em. And
even Kit Lukes won't give me a help—he
used to be d—d arbitrary and insolent,
but he would keep one going with a trifle,
but now he doesn't seem to care a straw
what happens to one. He's taken up so
much with Cecil Warleigh and his affairs,
that he doesn't seem to have interest in
anything else."

"Cecil Warleigh! I suppose the Grand
National broke him, and he's done for."

"'Deed he's not, though. He's very
much to the front is Captain Cecil
Warleigh; why, he claims the title and
estates, and every one says he'll get 'em.
Haven't you read about it? It's been in
the papers."

"How does he make his case out? I
thought it always went to the elder son;
and Sir John's father was Cecil War-

leigh's elder brother, and a fine fellow he
was too, one of the best-looking men
about town, though perhaps I shouldn't
say it."

"Oh, you knew him, did you? Well, he
appears to have been a queer lot, and
to have committed bigamy. When he
married Jack Warleigh's mother he had
another wife alive, a girl whom he married
down at Brighton."

Beamish gave a start, and stared hard
into the other's face.

"Brighton did you say?"

"Yes, Brighton, why not? She was a
barmaid, her name was Matterson or
something like it, and it is said there is
no doubt about the first marriage, and
the fact that the woman was alive.
Augustus Cohen is the solicitor Cecil
Warleigh has gone to, and they say he is
cock-sure of winning the case. Confound the fellow's luck. It was bad
enough losing the race, but it was comfort to think that Cecil Warleigh, who
puts on a lot of side with me, was dead
broke and found out. He was down on
his luck the Monday after the race, but
then, just in the nick of time, this turns
up, and now he is full of swagger, denies
all charges that were made against him,
and swears he won a pot of money over

the Grand National. I know that is a
lie, and so do you, but he carries things
off with a high hand, and people believe
him, or at least say they do.   I am pretty
sure that Kit Lukes is financing him and
lending him money."

Beamish listened to every word of Pat's
speech.   For a second or so, he seemed
to be thinking very gravely over it, then,
to the surprise of his companion, he
burst into a roar of laughter.

"So clever Mr. Kit thinks he has got
hold of a big thing, does he?" said
Beamish, laughing boisterously.

"You seem to find it very amusing, but
I don't see the joke, for it looks to me
as if Kit was about right.   You bet he'll
manage to get his claws into the estate if
Cecil Warleigh wins.   As for me, I ain't a
rich man, in fact, I am about as dead broke
as they make 'em, but I'd give a good bit
to see Master Kit sold, only it would
make him so cursed savage and nasty.
You needn't tell him I said so, though, not
that you're likely to, for I suppose you
ain't over thick just now?"

"No, we are not, but we shall be
partners again, though Mr. Lawyer
Lukes doesn't know it, and thinks that
he can chuck me aside like a worn-out
coat, now he doesn't want me," said

Beamish. " It's not like me to see others
making a lot out of me while I am
shunted."

Pat Considine stared at the Colonel,
and wondered what he was driving at, but
he was not destined to be enlightened, for
that gentleman appeared to be perfectly
contented with his own thoughts,
and did not take the slightest notice
of Pat's remarks. He was perfectly
careless about the " good thing" Pat
knew for Sandown the next day ; nor did
he seem to enjoy his sprightly conversation about races he had pulled, and turf
robberies he had been in ; but when it
came to the formula, without which that
honourable young man seldom took leave
of any one, "How was he off for
change?" he seemed quite relieved to
hear it, and produced half-a-sovereign
with the air of one who thought that
the luxury of being alone was cheap at
the price.

CHAPTER VI.

BEAMISH IS HIMSELF AGAIN.

FOR half an hour after Pat took his departure Beamish smoked and thought. Then he went upstairs and came down again, looking much more like the Colonel Beamish of his palmy days than he had since the Grand National. He wore his shiny tall hat, frock-coat, huge check trousers, and magnificent scarf-pin, instead of the modest suit of blue serge and billycock hat in which he sat and smoked in the bar-parlour of " The Old Lark Pie." His manner and gait seemed to have changed also, for the aggressive swagger had come back. The nod he gave to two customers of the house whom he met at the door, impressed them greatly.

" The Colonel has got a plant on. You see if he ain't. Mark my word, we shan't have him at 'The Pie' much longer. He'll be ownin' his 'osses agin, an' carryin' on with the best of 'em," said

one of the customers, as he watched the
gorgeous Colonel swaggering round the
corner of the court.

Since the disaster at Liverpool, he had
lived a bat-like life, seldom leaving the
grateful shade of the " Lark Pie " until
after dark ; but now he did not show any
of that desire to avoid the main thorough-
fares and thread devious back streets,
which is almost an instinct with broken
men ; and unabashed at the prospect of
meeting importunate bookmakers, he
made his way to a street off the Strand,
in which Mr. Lukes' office was situated.

" Say that some one wishes to see him
about Captain Warleigh's business,"
Beamish said to the clerk, who asked him
his name.

This procedure procured him a ready
admission to the inner sanctum, where
Mr. Lukes practised his profession.

" What, you ? " said Mr. Lukes, showing surprise rather than pleasure at seeing who his visitor was. " What do you
mean by bothering here, and sending me
a Tom Fool's message about a business
you know nothing about ? "

" Just what I said," answered Beamish,
lighting a cigar and seating himself in
the clients' chair. " I want to know why
I am shunted out of this, while you and

Warleigh cut it all up between you. I brought you and Warleigh together, we were partners, you and I, and we both came to grief over the Grand National. You manage to get up again, but you leave me smashed on the ground."

"It's nonsense to talk like that. How can we be partners when you have got nothing left? and what can you have to do with private business between Warleigh and me?" answered Lukes, looking somewhat nervously at Beamish. He was not at all desirous of having a row in his office, and he could imagine no reason why his late confederate should have called upon him, other than to offer him some violence. Beamish's expression, however, rather reassured him. He looked quite peaceable, and seemed to be enjoying the situation.

"I have done a good deal more for Captain Warleigh and you than either of you know of, and what I have done I mean to be paid for; I want to be in this 'plant' you have got up between you."

"There is the door, Colonel Beamish, I have something better to do than talk nonsense about things of which you can know nothing."

"Look here, Lawyer Lukes, it happens that I know more than you do. I was a witness of that marriage down at Brighton on which you stand to win Captain Warleigh's case."

Mr. Lukes laughed to himself now he saw Beamish's notion. He had evidently jumped to the conclusion that the case was fraudulent, and it had occurred to him that he might turn a dishonest penny by offering to go into the box to commit perjury. Lukes was surprised at the coolness of the offer, and felt half-amused and half-indignant at the other thinking him capable of engaging in such a clumsy fraud.

"Thank you. When I want any one to come and commit perjury for me I'll remember your name. In Captain Warleigh's case we have no need of that sort of evidence."

"Don't go so quick. I never suggested going into the box, but I was at that wedding safe enough. I ain't likely to forget. I can see Mrs. Butlin and Sam Butlin now, and the parson, a grey-haired man with a big nose, and poor Sally the bride. It ain't likely I shall ever forget the scene. I was there safe enough. They wouldn't have got on over well without me."

"Who has been taking the trouble to tell you all this?" asked Lukes. "I

don't know and I don't care, but we can
do without your evidence, for the witnesses whose name you mention, with the
pew-opener, were the only persons
present."

Beamish had dipped a pen into an
ink-pot and was writing something on an
envelope he had picked up.

" Can't make much of it now," he said,
as he threw what he had written across
to the lawyer.

" What fool's trick are you at ? "
answered the lawyer, after staring at
what Beamish had written on the
envelope, and had thrown it back
again.

" I could do that signature a good deal
better years ago, when I wrote it in the
register of St. James', at Brighton. Ah !
I thought I would move you, Kit Lukes,"
he added, as he saw the lawyer start and
change colour. " At that time my nose
hadn't been smashed in, I was tolerably
handsome and smart-looking in those
days—so, at least, a good many of the
women thought—and curiously enough
I was just the double of a man who was
said to be the handsomest man about
town : that was Captain John Warleigh.
I wasn't much more than twenty then,
but I had learned to look after myself,

for I had had a pretty hard time. When I had been mistaken once or twice for Captain Warleigh, I felt proud of the likeness, and thought that instead of being a poor beggar, who had to pick up a living as a billiard-marker, I'd have done a deal better as the Captain. May-be it was thinking like that, or may-be it was finding myself out of a job that started me off at a dangerous game, but, anyhow, I took to personating the Captain every now and again. I was clever with my pen in those days, and a party I knew got me a copy of the Captain's signature, and I wrote out a cheque or two in his name. They were changed, all of them, and, so far as I know, no fuss was ever made, and I determined to go in on a big scale. I went down to Brighton dressed up as a big swell, and called myself Captain Warleigh. First day I was there, something happened that I never counted on. I went into a tidyish-looking public-house to take a drink, and there, standing behind the bar, was a girl with whom I fell head-over-ears in love. She smiled and seemed to recognize me, and I saw that she mistook me for Captain Warleigh. She was a cleverish girl in her way, was Sally. But she had her head

stuffed full of nonsense she had read in
novels, and it seemed to her quite right
that a swell like Captain Warleigh should
marry a girl like her. Well, it all came
round as she hoped. 'The Captain'
hung round the bar all day long, and
after a week or two proposed marriage,
'Captain Warleigh' all the time. I
gave up the 'plant' I came down on, I
only passed one small cheque just to
cover expenses, for I was too afraid of
getting into trouble and having to run
away and so lose Sally. Well, we were
married, and it was some time before
Sally found out the trick I'd played.
She cut up pretty rough when she
did, you bet. But she stuck to me.
About that time England got a little
warm for me, and I skipped off to
America, and Sally followed me, and died
out there; and that's the end of the
story.

"Now, Kit Lukes, you see I could not
give evidence for your side about the
wedding, but I would be an uncommon
awkward witness against you."

Mr. Lukes' face had lengthened as he
listened to his story. Though he had no
exaggerated opinion of the Colonel's
regard for the truth, he began to be convinced that the story he had heard was

a true one. After all, it was far more
probable than the one they were setting
up on behalf of Cecil Warleigh's claim,
namely, that John Warleigh had, with
hardly any motive, committed a cold-
blooded and heartless bigamy.

"Awkward witness—why, whether they
believed you or not, one thing is certain,
that as soon as you left the box, you
would be taken into custody. If your
story is true, no one is likely to be afraid
of you giving evidence. The best
thing you can do, is to forget all about
it."

"Yes, and see you and Warleigh
making a lot out of what I did, while
I don't make a blessed penny-piece.
No, that ain't likely."

"I don't believe your story, and nobody else would, but if it were proved
to be true, you would end your days,
most likely, in prison. When you made
it up, you only thought how it would
affect our case, not of how it would
affect you," said Mr. Lukes, getting
up and walking to the door to open
it.

"That's where you go wrong, you think
that everybody but yourself is a fool,"
said Beamish, leaning back in his chair,
and showing no intention of going. "It

ain't likely I haven't thought how it would affect me."

"Did you take the trouble to learn what sentence you would be likely to get? Penal servitude for life, or perhaps fourteen years : the former for choice is my forecast. Now, take my tip, forget all about this silly story, and, if I were you, I'd clear out of the country. For old friendship's sake I could manage to pay your passage out anywhere, and give you a cheque—say for fifty pounds."

"Thanks for your liberal offer, which is gratefully declined, and I won't waste any more of your time. I have to find out who Sir John Warleigh's lawyers are, if possible, in time to see them this afternoon. By the way, you might tell me."

"Messrs Grimshaw, New Square, Lincoln's Inn," answered Mr. Lukes, who was no mean proficient at the game of bluff.

Neither spoke as Beamish walked to the door.

"In fourteen years you will be pretty nearly seventy, and I believe the air of Portland and Dartmoor is healthy, though the life there is not said to be conducive to old age. Penal servitude for life is only twenty-five years, as, after that term, the convict is generally released ; to a man of your age, however, that point is of no consequence," said the lawyer, as Beamish touched the handle of the door.

"Tell me something I don't know. If the other side can't win this case without putting me in the box, after I have put 'em on the track, they will lose it. I fancy I shall be worth a little more than fifty pounds to them."

In the drawer of the office table there was a loaded revolver, which Lukes had kept there since one occasion when he had been severely horse-whipped by a grateful client. It flashed through his mind that he might shoot Beamish, and declare he acted in self-defence. Most people would believe him. The idea was delicious, but —impossible.

"Beamish, old boy, why should two pals quarrel?" said Kit Lukes, putting on the sham good-fellow-manner, which he often used very efficaciously with men who did not know him, and who thought him a bluff, frank fellow, "sit down, and let's talk this out. After all, what you may get won't come out of my pocket."

CHAPTER VII.

COUNSEL'S OPINION.

As the day for the trial of the case of Warleigh *v.* Warleigh came nearer, every one on the side of the plaintiff became more and more confident.

"We have a complete case—that is to say, a fairly complete one," said Mr. Augustus Cohen, a day or two before the trial was to come on, to Cecil Warleigh, who had called on him at his office, "of course, if everything was too pat, I should look at it with suspicion. As it is, we have the landlady of the house where Captain and Mrs. Warleigh lived after the marriage. She identifies a portrait of Captain Warleigh, and says that he was very often away, that he was a handsome, gentlemanly man, and, from what she saw, she formed the impression that he had married beneath him. She always says she had an idea that there was something wrong between them, as now and then they quarrelled rather bitterly. At times she felt doubtful whether they were married, but Mrs. Warleigh on one occasion showed her a marriage certificate. She further says, that for the last six months Mrs. Warleigh lodged in her house the Captain never came there. Her evidence proves Mrs. Warleigh was alive and living in the house at the time of the second marriage. Then there is the servant of the lodgings, now an inmate of the Kensington Workhouse; she swears much to the same."

"It occurs to me that after all there might have been something wrong about that marriage," said Cecil, thoughtfully.

"Well, if there was, it will be for the other side to prove it, and you can set your mind at rest that there is nothing to suggest anything wrong. Sarah Matterson's previous history seems perfectly clear and straightforward—barmaid at the 'Regent's Head,' and daughter of the landlord of that house—what on earth was there to have prevented her from making a perfectly binding marriage?"

"How did you find Mrs. What's-her-name—landlady of the lodgings?" asked Cecil.

Mr. Augustus Cohen stroked his moustache, looked preternaturally shrewd, as

he debated in his own mind whether he
should disclose his source of information,
which really reflected no particular credit
on his sagacity or the ability with which
the case had been got up in his office.

As a matter of fact, Mr. Kit Lukes had
found out these witnesses. On the whole,
he thought it advisable to give the credit
of the discovery where it was due.

" He is a wonderful man, is your friend
Mr. Lukes. He seems to know as much
about the case as if he were in communi-
cation with the late Mrs. Warleigh," he
said, after he had told Cecil from whom
he obtained the information.

"Lukes is not my friend," answered
Cecil, "I hardly know anything about
him."

Mr. Cohen stroked his moustache and
looked into Cecil's face. He fancied that
he could form a very good estimate of the
relations that existed between him and
Mr. Lukes.

" There is one little thing about Mrs.
Gibling," he continued, " as a rule she
failed to remember dates, could not swear
when Captain Warleigh was at her lodgings, and when he wasn't, to a day or so—
but she did stick to one date, a Christmas
Day. He dined there one Christmas Day.
Now that is rather a critical point, for

the other side might prove that Captain Warleigh was somewhere else altogether on Christmas Day. Such a point as that could never do us much good, at the same time it might smash us."

There was a knock at the door, and a clerk came in with something written on a piece of paper.

" Ah, it's Dubbing, the expert in hand-writing. Better stay and hear what he says, Captain Warleigh, not that it is much more than a matter of form, for experts in hand-writing always say what they are expected to say by the side that calls them."

Mr. Dubbing was a stout, elderly man, whose great point was his manners. Amongst savage tribes he would have made a fortune as witch-doctor or medi-cine man. He probably had a near escape of becoming a medium, for he had that assumption of supernatural power which is required in spiritualistic circles. As it was, circumstances had made him an expert in hand-writing.

" This is Captain Warleigh," said Mr. Cohen, in response to the glance of mis-trust with which Mr. Dubbing regarded the third party, who was to hear a re-hearsal of his evidence.

" Very fortunate ; for I daresay he is

interested in hearing my verdict. It is very short and simple—namely, that the entry in the register was written by the same hand that penned the various specimens of hand-writing I have handed to me for the purpose of comparing with it," said Mr. Dubbing, with an air of having once for all settled the question.

"How about cross-examination? Can they make much out of it?"

"Who is on the other side as an expert? Not that I am afraid," answered Mr. Dubbing.

"There is Burrage, they are sure to have him," answered Mr. Cohen. "I suppose he will attack the hand-writing."

"I suppose that is what he will be there for; but, bless you, Burrage never has much to say; and he can be asked about half-a-dozen cases where he went wrong. He won't suggest anything that I can't answer," said Mr. Dubbing.

"Well, that's all satisfactory, you go into the next room and let my clerk take your proof; cut it as short as you can," said Mr. Cohen, whom experience had taught to look upon a professional expert as rather less reliable than any one else on the question of hand-writing.

"Mr. Dubbing is worth as much as Burrage, and *vice versâ*. But that point about the cheque is worth a hundred expert witnesses," he added, after Mr. Dubbing had left the room.

" What do you think about the case, Mr. Cohen ? " asked Warleigh.

" Well, it is my well-known custom not to say what I think, unless it is not worth fighting at all, but I will say this much— that I think I could beat old Grimshaw of New Square, on about half as strong a case, even if he had something very strong on his side. He is just the man to miss bringing out a point, even if there is one. I wonder who he will retain. As likely as not old Fumble. It is always about even money that a solicitor who is not worth his salt will retain Fumble. Now, our having Shebeen is a great thing in our favour, but I doubt if he will do us as much good as Fumble being on the other side will. Talking about Shebeen, it is about time for us to be off to his chambers."

Mr. Shebeen, Q.C., M.P., had been the most brilliantly successful of the many plucky young Irishmen of his day who had crossed St. George's Channel with brave hearts, a spare shirt or two, and a few pounds in their pockets, to herd together in top sets in the Temple, until they were called to the bar, and the base Saxon hired their glib tongues.

A born orator, he had made himself
a great lawyer, while no one was
more skilled in the art of advocacy. He
knew a law court as the pugilist of the
old time knew a fighting ring, and was
as well able to make and take every
advantage over an opponent in his arena.
His appearance was somewhat in his
favour, for he had a mobile, intellectual
face, and a good figure, and though his
manner was somewhat vulgar and under-
bred, it became impressive and dignified
as soon as he put on his wig and silk gown.

Warleigh, as soon as he saw him,
expressed the same satisfaction that he
would feel on seeing that the crack jockey
was going to ride a horse he had backed.
It was impossible for him to say how
much it was in his favour, but he believed
it would be a great deal, if it came to a
close finish.

"Think we have met before. Don't
you remember when Bamborough and I
lunched on your drag at Aldershot races?
A very pleasant day we had, and a very
good lot there were. I knew a good
many of your regiment well—-Lomond
and several others: there is no regiment,
except the Guards, in which I have so
many friends," Mr. Shebeen said, as
he shook Warleigh's hand. He continued to talk in this strain for some

time, for though he was a busy man, he generally found time to air his late acquired knowledge of smart people, whenever an opportunity offered.

Cecil Warleigh, who had only heard of him out of his profession, as a sturdy Radical member of Parliament, was sufficiently versed in the ways of politicians to be no whit surprised at this characteristic. When he began to talk business, however, all that was mean and ridiculous about him vanished. Cecil Warleigh admired the way in which he grasped the salient points of the case, and waited anxiously to hear him express some opinions.

Mr. Shebeen was very guarded in this ; it depended upon what the other side could do in the way of disproving the case for the plaintiff. As it stood, it was undoubtedly strong.

" Well, it is a very unpleasant thing to have to wash so much dirty family linen in public," said Cecil. As it had become more and more clear to him that he was the rightful owner to a fine estate, he had begun to feel quite satisfied with himself again, and to forget the unpleasant circumstances of the last month or two. Still, as he spoke, he found himself wondering how much of the recent scandal about the Grand National had reached the ears of his audience.

" Your remark does you credit," answered Shebeen, who had heard all about the Grand National, and believed the worst, but thought that it was a matter about which society would not think harshly, if he won his case. But after all, who among us belonging to a decent family, has not got some member of it of whom he has cause to be a little ashamed?

Mr. Shebeen was descended from the Irish Kings, but there was a hiatus in his pedigree for the dozen generations or so preceding his father. His immediate ancestor belonged to a class that is peculiarly prolific in begetting Irish patriots, orators and statesmen. He had been a small shop-keeper and "gombeen" man—a peasant's money-lender.

"Shall I meet you at Lady Lion-hunter's reception, Cohen?" said Shebeen, as the lawyer and his client were leaving his chambers.

"No, I dine at Greenwich with Lord Tiburn. It's to be a very jolly friendly little party," answered the lawyer, with an assumed air of nonchalance.

"What d——d low people get into society! When I come by my own, I'll take care who I know," thought Cecil, as he walked down the Strand.

CHAPTER VIII.

WARLEIGH *v.* WARLEIGH: CASE FOR PLAINTIFF.

THE case of Warleigh *v.* Warleigh went
through all its preliminary stages with
less than the average amount of stop-
pages. Pleadings were duly drawn.
Interrogations were administered and ob-
jected to, allowed, appealed against,
allowed again, and at length answered
without bringing the case any further in
the end, one way or the other. Opinions,
on evidence, were written, advising the
solicitor who knew much better than the
counsel who wrote them as to what
evidence ought to be forthcoming. The
case was set down for trial; briefs were
delivered for counsel, and on the first
day of the assizes at Fetchester, after
the jury were duly sworn, Mr. Eldon
Stookes—the junior counsel for the plaintiff, having hurriedly written on the back
of his brief, " At the Fetchester Summer
Assizes, before Mr. Justice Snoozley and

a special jury. Warleigh *versus* War-
leigh. For the Plaintiff, Shebeen, Q.C.,
Topper, Q.C., Lumberg, and Eldon
Stookes. For the Defendant, Fumble,
Q.C., and Percy Slant "—stood up and
opened the pleadings.

Never before had the Civil Court at
Fetchester been so crowded. The cases
that were usually set down for trial were
of a perfectly humdrum and uninteresting
character. At last, here was a case being
tried in the sleepy little town which was
discussed all over England. Members
of county families crowded the galleries
of the court. Several noblemen, among
them Lord Bamborough, who was chair-
man of the Grand Jury, and many ladies of
position in the county, had been provided
with seats on the Bench. The good people at Fetchester crowded the court, and
a constant shower of cards, begging for
places, poured in on the High Sheriff.
Amongst the press, there were one or
two faces well known in London—war
correspondents out of work, and graphic
writers—who, as there was nothing more
interesting going on just then, were not
unwilling to write a descriptive report of
the great case of Warleigh v. Warleigh.
The barristers never mustered very strong
at Fetchester, the very small calendar of

prisoners for trial, which the Judges generally allude to, in their charges to the
Grand Jury, as so very gratifying a circumstance, has made the town stink in
their nostrils. Some of them stay there
for a day or two, because they enjoy the
scenery on the sluggish river, and the
pleasant quiet of the streets. One of these
was Jack Langford, a briefless barrister,
who took the enforced idleness of his life
with a philosophic resignation, and who
had learnt to look upon sitting in a court of
law, doing nothing but drawing caricatures, as a magnificent career in life,
hoping, on grounds insufficient enough,
that it would some day lead to an
appointment, and a provision for his
old age. Finding himself at Fetchester
on this occasion, he set himself down to
two or three days' hard work, at depicting
the various celebrities in court.

"Tell you what I will do, Sheep, old
chap," says Lord Bamborough, digging
old Sheepington, the High Sheriff, in the
ribs, "I'll take you a thousand to two
hundred against Jack Warleigh, or I'll
lay you a thousand to two fifty."

Mr. Sheepington, whose mind con-
tinually dwells on the expenses his honourable office has put him to, shudders at this
light talk about money.

"Well, as you like, it is not a great catch any way—they all say it is a moral for Cecil Warleigh, but I don't think he looks too confident. It's my opinion that there is a 'ramp' on somehow, and I'd take sixty-six to one, if it were kicking about, that old Cecil finds himself at Dartmoor, with his hair cut ; and a tasty thing in brown dittos provided for him by a grateful country, before it is all over."

"'Pon my word, Bamborough, I hardly think there are grounds for saying that. It's a painful affair, very painful ; but if Cecil Warleigh does win the case, I consider that the country will accept him in the position in which the law of the land places him ; I shall feel bound to take that line."

"I'll tell him that. It will be the one thing that will reconcile him to his painful duty of turning his nephew out, and getting into his place."

"I shall be glad if you will do so," answered Mr. Sheepington, solemnly, and then he turned the conversation to his grievances as a High Sheriff.

"Very bad, I daresay, but I must be off, and hear Cecil Warleigh's man do his work. He has that Irishman—Shebeen. I have met him at Newmarket ; a vulgar, pushing customer, but uncommon useful at his own game, so they tell me," said Bamborough, hurrying off.

"Hullo, old chappie, what price the wicked uncle who forged the register!" he cried out, as he came against Cecil Warleigh going into court.

"Confounded young ass," was Warleigh's mental remark, but he smiled and tried to look pleasant. Perhaps it was as well that Bamborough indulged in friendly chaff. He wondered what that young nobleman, who, at the bottom, was an uncommonly hard-headed young fellow, really thought.

The array of counsel for the prosecution was imposing. There was Mr. Shebeen, who had been brought down special, as he did not belong to the circuit; then Mr. Topper, because he was a good man, who could conduct the case in a satisfactory manner, should anything happen to Mr. Shebeen. Mr. Lumberg was somewhat of a phenomenon, a stupid Jew; or rather, perhaps, a Jew who was wise enough to see that it was not worth while to work hard about other people's affairs, in order to make very little money for himself. He was a near relative of Mr. Augustus Cohen's, and obtained a certain number of briefs from him in the course of the year. Mr. Eldon Stookes

was put in the case as a second junior,
because Mr. Lumberg was really of no
use, even when he took the trouble to
keep awake. Mr. Cohen was right in his
prophesy. Mr. Grimshaw of Lincoln's
Inn had retained Mr. Fumble, Q.C. The
selection was a natural one enough, as he
was the leader of the circuit, and in
many respects was a man whose name
would be likely to occur to a solicitor with
a leading brief to give away in an important case. A horse-dealer—for whom
Mr. Fumble had once appeared in a
warranty case, afterwards described his
learned counsel as a "flat catcher," and
the story getting about amongst the bar,
the description was recognized as a
happy one. As a young man he had
been very successful at sessions, and as a
defender of prisoners had been fairly
effective. To hear him cross-examine a
few witnesses, and afterwards reply to
the case for the prosecution, would sometimes throw the clearest-headed people
into confusion. The muddle he got into
himself, would become contagious, and
the jury in sheer despair would sometimes acquit a prisoner whose guilt had
been clearly proved. In after life,
interest, good temper, handsome presence,
a pleasing voice, and that sort of

eloquence which consists in an abundant supply of sonorous platitudes and hack quotations, gained for him a good place at the bar. He had probably lost more verdicts that might have been won than any man in the profession; still, he had plenty of admirers. "That is the man for my money," would be the opinion of some pleased listener to his orations, in a case which it was not possible for him to lose.

Mr. Shebeen eyed his learned friend superciliously as he said "good morning." He had considerable contempt for him, mixed with an uneasy feeling that Fumble, who was a gentleman by birth, had something about him which he, Shebeen, did not possess. "Idiotic prejudice, humbug, that no reasonable man cared twopence about," Shebeen snarled to himself contemptuously; but for all that, he felt bitter about it, and comforted himself by making mental notes for future Radical speeches at public meetings, and in the House, and for swaggering talk in private life, about his friends Bamborough and Lomond.

Mr. Percy Slant was perhaps in his own line one of the strongest men at the bar. His line was case law. His mind was a very dictionary of the names of

decided cases, he knew their names, and
the pages of the reports in which they were
to be found, and he had a fair grasp of
the principles of law on which they were
decided. He could hardly take any
interest in a case that was simply a
question of evidence and fact ; and since
he had failed to find what he called a
" point " in Warleigh v. Warleigh, to
tell the truth, he began to feel that the
business was one rather beneath a man of
his ability. He was a little, prematurely-
old-looking man, with a short face and
large eyes, and had an owlish look of
wisdom and dignity. He was always a
favourite junior with family lawyers like
Mr. Grimshaw.

" Ah, I'm glad we have him, he is one
of the least objectionable of 'em—never
opens his mouth except to snore, till it's
time for him to sum up," Mr. Shebeen
whispered to his junior, staring at Mr.
Justice Snoozley so as to leave no doubt
in his lordship's mind that he was the
subject of some more or less ill-natured
remark ; for Mr. Shebeen retaliated for
some kicks and snubs he had had to bear
in early life, by being habitually insolent
to the Bench, with two or three excep-
tions, of whom he was afraid. Giving his
gown a hitch, Mr. Shebeen got up and

opened the case. He was quiet, impressive and clear, showing the jury what he was going to prove, and how he was going to prove it. The story, painful and extraordinary though it was, was undoubtedly true. There was not the slightest possible room for doubt that Captain John Warleigh had married Sarah Matterson. Mrs. Butlin, who was present at the wedding, had seen Captain Warleigh on several occasions when he was quartered at Brighton, and she was certain that he was the man who used to come to the " Regent's Head " after Sarah Matterson, whom he afterwards married. Samuel Butlin, who had seen Captain Warleigh at cricket, gave similar evidence. The matter of the hand-writing in the register and the cheque passed by Captain Warleigh to Mrs. Butlin were also dwelt upon. " The latter fact, gentlemen, proves conclusively the identity of the man who married Sarah Matterson," said Mr. Shebeen, coming to an impressive pause. The next point in the case was whether or no Sarah Matterson was alive to the time of the second marriage. Upon this question Mr. Shebeen laid a good deal of stress, as if he thought it would be the point in his case, at which the defence would

direct their attack. Mr. Cohen's bright
eyes gave a twinkle of intelligence. Mr.
Fumble was just the man to be led away
by such an artifice as that, though it
was not a particularly deep one. Mr.
Shebeen hardly made the most of his
facts, and a less skilled solicitor than Mr.
Augustus Cohen might have been disgusted at the halting manner in which
that part was opened. Mr. Cohen
laughed to himself as he noticed from
Mr. Fumble's expression that he evidently
was struck with the weakness of the
opening on this point.

The evidence for the plaintiff was long,
and not particularly interesting. Mrs.
Butlin made a very fair witness; her
cross-examination only made it very clear
to the jury that she had not the slightest
doubt of the identity of Captain Warleigh of the Lancers and the man who
married Sarah Matterson.

" How often did I see him? Why,
every day and all day, for pretty near
three weeks, sitting in the parlour of the
' Regent's Head.' "

" Then you swear that Captain Warleigh was in your house every day for
three weeks before the date of the
marriage."

The artistic briefless barrister was

drawing a caricature of Mr. Augustus
Cohen, and looking just then rather
hard at the eminent lawyer,. he noticed
a twitch in the muscles under his eye,
and a nervous pulling at his moustache.

" Mr. Cohen doesn't seem to like that,"
thought the briefless one to himself.
" Fumble seems to be on dangerous
ground for the plaintiff," but Mr. Fumble,
if he were on dangerous ground, seemed
as ignorant of it as some child playing at a game blindfolded.

" No, sir, I won't swear any such thing
after all these years, and me having
no reason to remember particular, and
having plenty of my own affairs to think
of," answered Mrs. Butlin.

Mr. Cohen looked relieved.

" Fumble has been very hot," thought
Langford, as he sharpened his pencil and
watched Mr. Cohen's face. Fumble went
on with his cross-examination, like some
unwieldy barge on the lower Thames,
following the course of the tide, bumping
irresponsibly against anything that came
in the way. Soon he was cold again, and
Mr. Cohen's face showed no more appre-
hension. Altogether Mrs. Butlin was a
very good witness. The cross-examination
had been so long, and dealt with so many
*un*important details, that the minds of the

jury were diverted from the important point, namely, that her knowledge of Captain Warleigh was a very slight one indeed before the time he became a customer at the Regent's Head. A great deal of cross-examination was directed to show that she was mistaken in the identity of Sarah Matterson with the person she saw in London. On this point, however, she was not to be shaken at all. There seemed very little doubt that either she was perjuring herself, which somehow no one believed, or that her evidence was correct.

Sam Butlin's evidence was pretty much the same as his wife's, and it was not touched in cross-examination. After that came the point about the cheque. It was proved conclusively by several witnesses from banks, that the cheque drawn by the alleged Captain Warleigh was paid by the real Captain Warleigh's bankers, and that no trouble was ever made about it. Then came Mr. Dubbing, the expert in hand-writing, and the rest of the day was occupied in a foggy cross-examination about up-strokes and down-strokes, and the way the "r" in Warleigh was written. Mr. Fumble was certainly in his element in this, and several of the jury followed the example of Mr. Justice Snoozley and went fast asleep.

" I will put it to you shortly. Are you convinced that those letters are in the same hand-writing as that of the register?" asked Mr. Shebeen in re-examination.

The witness had some letters in his hand which were admitted to have been written by Captain John Warleigh.

" Puffectly, puffectly convinced," wheezed Dubbing the expert.

" And I take it that you will swear that the entry in the register was written by Captain Warleigh who wrote these letters," said Mr. Shebeen, with an air of great gravity. " He'd swear the same of the runic inscriptions if I put it to him, I believe," he added in a whisper to Mr. Topper, Q.C.

" I object to that question, as being an improper one to put to a witness; for what he is asked is the point which the jury has to decide," said Mr. Fumble, jumping up, like a Jack-in-the-box.

Then there was a legal argument about the form of the question, in which Mr. Slant distinguished himself, but which dropped when Mr. Justice Snoozley, on thoroughly waking up, pointed out, as was obviously the case, that it was not of the slightest practical importance to either side.

Certainly, for the plaintiff, the case was being proved up to the hilt.

CHAPTER IX.

IN THE SCALES OF JUSTICE.

"WHAT an infernal blackguard that fellow Warleigh must have been!" was the opinion expressed very freely and unanimously in the robing-room.

"There is one man who doesn't believe in the case for the plaintiff," said Jack Langford, the caricaturist, to Mr. Percy Slant, whom he had once known very well, before the one had distinguished himself, and the other had obviously failed. Mr. Slant did not take the trouble to reply. What was the good of talking about anything to a man who probably did not know what was the rule in Shelly's case, or what were the principles that guided the judges in Fletcher *v.* Rylands, and who probably would draw caricatures placidly through the most interesting of legal arguments.

"It's the solicitor for the plaintiff. I

watched the expression of his face when Fumble was cross-examining that woman; he is afraid that you will pin them down to some particular day when their Captain Warleigh was at Brighton, and then prove an *alibi*," continued Langford, as he put on his hat and walked away.

Mr. Slant shook his head pityingly.

" Poor chap, he has not the remotest chance of ever getting into work—' the expression of Cohen's face,'—did ever man hear such nonsense—' prove an *alibi*,'—why, he seems to think he is at the Middlesex Sessions," said Mr. Slant to some other men who had heard the conversation ; and then he went away to attend a droning consultation with his learned leader. To tell the truth, they, all three, disbelieved in their case. Mr. Grimshaw, though out of principle he did not refuse to take it—and mismanage it, disliked litigious business, and felt that misfortune to a certain extent would serve his client right. Mr. Fumble complacently thought of the eloquent speech he would make for the defence. Captain Warleigh's death in the Crimea, though it had nothing particularly to do with the case, would give him a grand chance for some well turned sentences of

commonplace. Mr. Slant had a point of
law that he hoped to get in somehow or
the other. Even Slant thought it was
of no importance and would not affect the
verdict ; still to hear it argued, and made
as he intended to do, ought almost to
make up to his client for losing the case.
Jack Warleigh was present, and as he
listened to his learned advisers drearily
maundering away for half an hour, the dis-
tressing conviction forced itself upon him,
that in this crisis of his life he had fallen
among fools. This same misfortune has
happened to more men who have gone to
law than is commonly believed. It is
not the case, as is vulgarly supposed, that
all lawyers are knaves.

On the second day of the trial, the
case for the plaintiff was concluded.
Only on one occasion did Langford—who
had nothing better to do, and so watched
the case to the end—catch that look of
anxiety on Mr. Cohen's face. It was in
the examination of Mrs. Gibling, the
landlady of the lodgings where Sarah
Matterson had gone after her marriage.

" You say that Captain Warleigh came
only to the lodgings on a few occasions
after the 1st of June, 1852? the date of
the second marriage, my lord," asked
Mr. Fumble.

" Now, my good woman, what makes you so certain about that ? "

" Don't ' good woman ' me, for I won't bear it from you," answered the witness, who had been in a court of justice before, and had a general notion that counsel on the other side ought to be treated with insolence. Mr. Cohen looked a little worried, they were on dangerous ground. If the cross-examiner did not stumble on to something else, he might put his hands on the weak point of the case.

" But I am sure, Mrs. Gibling, you are a good woman," said Fumble, and at that brilliant joke there was a roar of laughter which woke up the learned judge.

" Really, Mr. Fumble, I think it would be as well not to push this any further," he remarked. He had not the slightest notion what it was that Mr. Fumble was pushing, but he felt irritated at being disturbed.

Mr. Fumble did not know either, but the landlady was determined to answer his question and give him a facer.

" I remembers it becos' on the occasion when he came afterwards—it was Christmas Day. It was the first Christmas dinner as Gibling ever eat in that house, and we 'oped the lodgers would

dine hout, but they didn't, so that's how
I remembers, for Christmas Day is—or
leastwise, used to be arter the first of
June," said the good lady, with great
volubility and great exasperation—then
suddenly she caught the eye of Mr.
Cohen, and at once came to a stop.
" I can't say, of course, as it wer'
Christmas Day, it wer' a day when
Gibling an' me 'ad my dear mar to
dinner, an' that might have been enny
day."

" By Gad ! if he sticks to her there, he
will win the case. You must know where
your man was on Christmas Day, and
she's certain enough in her own mind
about it," said Jack Langford—who was
drawing an imaginary picture of the
learned judge, in an advanced stage of
intoxication—to the junior for the
defence.

It was a strange thing, but for once
Mr. Slant instead of being vexed, received the gratuitous piece of advice, and
pulling at his leader's gown, he whispered into his ear.

" I wish you would sit down, sir," said
Mr. Fumble techily ; " you put me out in
the thread of my cross-examination,
which you must allow me to conduct un-
interrupted." What the thread of Mr.

Fumble's cross-examination was, no one on earth ever knew, but that was the remark he invariably did make to a junior, who ventured a suggestion. Having made it, he seemed to swing round with the tide, and bumping along, he drifted away to other points, and Mr. Cohen looked thoroughly satisfied with himself and his case again.

Mr. Fumble's opening speech was an oration which his admirers long remembered. " That's the old school of forensic eloquence—reminds me of the late Sir Hustleton Bustleton, whom I once heard in court," Grimshaw, who was delighted with it, remarked to Jack Warleigh.

Jack didn't altogether think that a description of his father's death at Balaclava, or a recitation of part of ' The Charge of the Light Brigade,' really would do much good to anyone, except to the learned judge whom it lulled to sleep again. He had been woke up by the sound of carts outside the Court-house, which had made him extremely irritable and unpleasant for some little time. When Fumble came to speak of Mrs. Warleigh, he really was eloquent and impressive. He had seen her, and, as he spoke, he was haunted by the look of sorrow and indignation that had come into her gentle face when she spoke of the shameful charge they had brought against her husband. She thought little of the shame it would bring upon herself, for she did not believe in the possibility of her not having been a wife in point of law, nor did she care so much about her son's loss of riches and position, for they often caused little real happiness. But that her brave, dead soldier husband should have his fair fame smirched by such a shameful accusation, seemed to her to be a wrong and injustice too horrible to succeed. Fumble had understood her feelings, for he was a gentleman and a kindly hearted man, and as Helen Warleigh's advocate he became eloquent.

"The jury would see the lady whom Captain Warleigh—a brave and honourable man, who had lived and died as a gentleman should—was accused of bringing this shame upon. Their case was a negative one, at that length of time it was impossible to prove where John Warleigh was on the day he was said to have married Sarah Matterson, but he hoped he should show them that the plaintiff had not proved that he had made that marriage, and that if he had, Sarah Matterson was not alive on the day he had married again. It was monstrous to believe that this brave hero of whom they, as Loamfordshire men—as Englishmen—had a right to be proud, had tricked the lady about to be placed in the box into becoming his mistress instead of his wife." Mr. Fumble subsided, with the true forensic ' snort and plump,' into his seat, and was satisfied that he had made a striking speech. And perhaps he had, but Mr. Shebeen, as he blew his nose, seeming somehow to infuse a contemptuous note into that operation, thought to himself that his learned friend had said nothing that he could not tear to bits in his reply. He had certainly opened no case which he had much reason to fear. To tell the truth, the defence had no case beyond criticism of that set up by the plaintiff. Mrs. Warleigh was one of their first witnesses. Mr. Fumble had called her because he wished the jury to see her, knowing that the sight of that gentle lady, full of implicit trust in the honour of her dead husband, would gain the sympathies of the jury, rather than because she was able to give any evidence that was important. She swore that her husband had spent the Christmas Day with her on which the landlady of the lodgings had sworn that her Captain Warleigh had dined at her house. Per-

haps even Mr. Fumble himself then saw
what a chance he had missed, but the opportunity was gone.   She swore that her
husband, except on one or two occasions,
when he was absent on military duty,
was never a whole day away from her.

" Your husband was absent once or
twice, then ? " asked Mr. Shebeen, in cross-
examination.

Yes, she remembered him being
absent one day, and she thought more
often.

" And he told you he had to be away
on duty ? " said Mr. Shebeen, looking at
the jury.   " I don't think, Mrs. Warleigh,
I need put you to the pain of answering
any other questions," he added, as he sat
down, with an air of manly chivalry.

" 'Ansom, very 'ansom," whispered one
of the jurymen to his neighbour, who did
not recognize the fact that there was
really nothing to cross-examine about.

Among the other witnesses there was
the expert in hand-writing Mr. Burrage,
he was as confident that the signature in
the register was a forgery as the expert
called for the plaintiff was to the contrary.
Mr. Fumble and he groped through a
maze of up-strokes and down-strokes
and curls of the W in Warleigh, and then
Mr. Shebeen took him in hand, but did

not make much of him, for, after the custom of his class, he became more and more positive. Among the other witnesses was old Major Chaffinch, who remembered the two months when John Warleigh was said to have been at Brighton. He was on leave then, and spent some of the time in London at Limmer's Hotel. He occasionally met his friend Warleigh, who was also on leave during that period — he believed he was staying in his chambers in St. James' Street.

"Now, Major Chaffinch, from what you know of the late Captain Warleigh, do you think he was a man who would commit bigamy, and deceive the lady we have seen to-day?" asked Mr. Fumble, with a fine disregard of the law of evidence.

Mr. Shebeen did not wake up the Judge and object. After all, Major Chaffinch could say nothing that would have any effect on the jury; for they would assume that he would not believe his friend capable of such a thing.

"No, sir, I don't. We weren't Josephs, begad in the Lancers, but there was not one of us who would have married a barmaid," was old Chaffinch's answer.

Mr. Shebeen congratulated himself on his self-restraint in not objecting. The

Major's answer gave him matter for some
very telling passages in his reply on the
whole case; in which he pointed out
that Captain Warleigh's intimate friend
seemed to think his having been guilty
of the folly of marrying a bar-maid was
the most improbable fact of the story as
told by the case for the plaintiff.

Mrs. Chaffinch was an interested reader
of the verbatim reports of this speech,
when it was in the Fetchester paper.

" What can be more contemptible than
an old man looking back and gloating
over the vices of his middle age ! When
Justinian and Julian read this, they will
blush with shame," she remarked as she
read the paper and made the most of
every word of sarcasm that had been
heaped upon her spouse. His evidence
certainly did not do the defence much
good, nor did that of General Cottingham,
or any of the others of the regiment that
were called, it only emphasized the fact
that it was quite impossible to disprove
the case for the plaintiff. Mr. Fumble
had nothing to say in his summing up,
that he had not said in his opening. Mr.
Shebeen replied ; and he tore to pieces
most of the argument that had been used
on the other side. " My learned friend
asked, ' Why did not Sarah Matterson

come forward and claim her rights?' Gentlemen, I am not going to waste time in speculating as to what was the fate of that unhappy and deeply wronged woman. She disappears, and leaves no trace behind her, and for years that shameful page in John Warleigh's life is closed. But to-day in this Court it is opened again. My friend appeals to your sentiments of pity for a lady in whose misfortune we all alike sympathize. Gentlemen, I appeal to your sense of justice, and submit that I have given proof which has not been in one iota refuted—that John Warleigh did marry Sarah Matterson, and that when he afterwards went through the ceremony of marriage with Helen Dalton, Sarah Matterson his lawful wife was alive."

The Judge's summing up was of that perfectly colourless character which some people approve of. "If the defendant was not the legitimate son of John Warleigh, the plaintiff would succeed in his action; if he were, he would not. If they believed the witnesses who swore that they knew John Warleigh, and saw him marry Sarah Matterson, and the witnesses who also swore to having seen Sarah Matterson alive after the date of the second mar-

riage, then the plaintiff had proved the
case. The defendant had called no
evidence to disprove this. The matter
of the cheque was of the greatest importance; it certainly tended to confirm the
evidence of identity. The experts as to
hand-writing were distinctly opposed. He
was bound to say that in such cases
there generally was a conflict of expert
evidence." Then he read all the notes
he had made, and it was surprising
how much he had taken down, con-
sidering the amount of sleep he had
got through. He seemed to read himself
to sleep, for his voice became more and
more drowsy, till at last he came to a stop.
As soon as the droning voice of the judge
ceased, there was a buzz of conversation
all over the Court; and every one began
to speculate about the verdict.

That it would be for the plaintiff, was
the general opinion. One or two people
suggested that the jury would not agree.

"That Irish beggar, Shebeen, romped
in, the other chap couldn't make him
gallop," said Bamborough to Mr. Sheepington, the High Sheriff.

Jack Warleigh, who sat under his
counsel, looked grim and savage.
He felt convinced that he had lost the
day; he could see that in the ex-

pressions of people who were looking at
him to see how he took it.

Mr. Grimshaw had no comfort to give
him, except that he considered that Mr.
Fumble's two speeches were remarkably
fine ones, and that he had no doubt that
if Mr. Shebeen had only tried to lead
certain evidence, which, as a matter of
fact, he never thought of leading, Mr.
Percy Slant's legal argument would have
been most effective; " for my part, I never
did court litigious business," he added, as
if his condescension in mismanaging his
affairs would make up for his client's
having to leave the Court without money
or name of his own.

" They ought to be in by this time,"
said Mr. Cohen to Cecil, as he looked at
his watch, " they have been out twenty
minutes. I don't like too much delay, it
looks like disagreeing. Ah ! here they
come. Well, Sir Cecil Warleigh, I think
I can congratulate you."

Half an hour afterwards a telegraph
boy climbed the stairs to Mr. Kit Lukes'
office. Beamish and Lukes, who had both
thought it desirable to keep away from
Fetchester, were sitting in the inner
office. On the table covered with
old briefs, that had become as dirty
as the cases set out in them, stood an

almost empty bottle of brandy and two glasses.

"Here's the winner," said Beamish, swallowing the contents of his glass, as he heard the sharp single knock at the outer door. Lukes snatched the brown envelope from the boy who brought it.

"It's all right, it's the plaintiff," said Kit Lukes, waving the telegram in the air.

CHAPTER X.

AFTER THE VERDICT.

VERDICT for the plaintiff. People in Court instinctively turned their eyes on Jack Warleigh. Have not human beings, the world over, a passion for seeing their fellows taking their punishment ? We are less brutal, perhaps, than our ancestors were, but, after all, do we not enjoy seeing a different kind of pain inflicted ? We do not crowd to see hangings, but we find criminal trials enjoyable. Dainty ladies will, day after day, stare from the bench, to which their rank gains them invitation, at some wretched being, of their own sex for choice, because they can more easily read all her agony, who is being tried for her life. Our gorge— if we are superior people—rises at the notion of a fairly-fought-out-to-the-end prize fight, but with what a keen enjoyment do we look on and listen to a damaging cross-examination, if we have the good luck to be present ! When the

wretched victim writhes in the box, as
blow after blow is struck him; blows
crueller than any that were ever dealt by
Sayers' right. We shrink from seeing
physical pain inflicted, because we know
that sooner or later some of it will come
back to us, but the refinements of the age
make us appreciate moral suffering.

Jack Warleigh took his reverse of
fortune well. Loss of position and
wealth did not at once seem very terrible. It was not his fault that they
were lost, and, for the moment, he felt
ready enough to fight his way in the
world without them. But his mother's
face told him what the verdict meant to
her. It did not for one moment shake
her faith in her husband, still she saw how
black a stain it had cast on his memory.

"Never mind what they say, your
father was as good and honourable as he
was brave. He never could have done
this," she said, holding up her head, as if
she wished to let every one in the Court
who saw her know that she felt no shame.

Cecil Warleigh crossed over to the side
where Jack sat, and held out his hand.

"You were good to me, Jack, when I
had nothing, I don't forget that. I will
see that you are all right."

Jack coloured up and looked uncomfortable.

" We cannot be friends. I don't want to judge you, but I say this is a conspiracy, and that you ought never to have come into Court."

" Haven't you heard what was sworn to you ? You can't expect me to be such a Quixotic fool as to forego my right in order to hush up a family scandal."

Jack turned away, and Cecil walked off, well content enough to leave matters as they were. He, at all events, had done the right thing.

Jack wished to say a word to Mr. Grimshaw, but that gentleman was very anxiously discussing a question about costs with his counsel, with all an attorney's interest in that most important question. And as, after all, there did not seem to be much gained by talking, he left the Court with his mother, and they walked home together to the little house in Fetchester where she still lived.

Jack talked to her about Kate. He could go up to London on the next day to see her. Of course he was ready to free her from her engagement, but he repeated how she had said to him that the lawyers should never rob him of her love. " I'll work hard at something or other, and win a fortune for her," he said, flushing with pride at the thought of Kate caring so much for him.

Mrs. Warleigh felt rather guilty. When Kate had stayed a few days with her, she had at first been fascinated, then repelled by her, and had been tempted to doubt whether or no she really loved Jack.

" If your loss shows you how true and loving she is, it will be easy enough to bear," she answered, looking with pride at her big son, and thinking that somehow he ought to fight his way in the world.

The next day, however, when Jack rang the bell of the little house in Kensington, General Cottingham himself, looking old and haggard, opened the door.

" Come in here, my dear boy," he said, as he led Jack into the dining-room, and pushed him into a big arm-chair ; " pull yourself together, for I have some bad news to tell you."

" What about ? Kate, she isn't ill ? "

" Yes, it's about Kate, but she is not ill. It was trying her too far, this confounded verdict. You can't expect anyone to be better than themselves, I suppose. Anyhow, she isn't, but here, you had better read her letter, which she left this morning—she writes straight to the point."

The writing seemed to swim before Jack's eyes, but he read the letter through, and it was not difficult to understand, for Kate certainly did write straight to the point.

She had gone away with Cecil Warleigh, and they would be married that morning. She had always loved Cecil, too well to marry anyone else. Still, if Jack had won the case, she would have married him, and done her best to have prevented his ever finding out that she was not in love with him, but it was best for him that things should be as they were.

Jack said nothing as he handed the letter back, but shook hands with the General and went away without saying another word. He will never know where he walked to, or how he spent the next three or four hours, except that he wandered aimlessly about like a man in a dream. He was roused from his forgetfulness by hearing a friendly voice calling out his name, and feeling some one grip his arm.

" Jack Warleigh, by Jupiter ! the very man I was thinking about. I have been reading your case in the papers this morning. Infernally bad luck for you, old boy ! You remember me, don't you ? Jones of St. George's."

Jack did not recall the name at first; then he remembered the man. It was

the freshman who had thrown the egg
at the proctor on that memorable evening,
that preceded the more memorable day,
when he learned that he had come into
the title and estates which he had just
lost.

"You remember that evening, don't
you? Well, they found out somehow that
I was one of the men in your rooms, and
they sent me down, and the governor
wouldn't let me come up again; best
piece of good luck that could have
happened to me. My governor gave me
up as a bad job, and I was sent out to
the Cape, with my passage paid, and a
hundred pounds; not much of a capital,
but with it I made my way to Kimberly.
I went into a digging venture in the
Bulfontein mine. My partner, as good
a fellow as ever stepped, believed in the
mine, which was almost abandoned in
those days, and was glad enough to take
me in with him for even the small capital
I had. Everything turned up trumps,
our claims paid, and we took up more
and more, till we have the best block in
the mine. The last two years have made
a man of me. It is the best place in the
world for making a pile. Not that everybody has as good luck as I did, still,
there are heaps of chances."

Jack remembered what a weedy nervous youngster the other had been, and noticed how strong and self-reliant he had become. "I'd like to follow your example," he said, "and get out of the country."

"Why shouldn't you? Look here, come and have luncheon and talk over things. I have to be in the city in an hour. I'm going out again to-morrow," said Jones, who, taking Jack's arm, made for a restaurant.

He was not, perhaps, so very much wiser than he had been at college, and owed his success to good luck, rather than anything else. Still he was just the sort of companion to do Jack good.

The latter began to forget his troubles as he ate his luncheon and listened to Jones' talk about the strange life of the diamond fields.

Yes, he thought he would have gone out there himself, and tried to win a fortune, if Kate had only been true to him.

"Don't be afraid of South Africa. If you come to the diamond fields, you'll find a lot of adventurers; we don't pretend to be anything else; but every one will be glad to see you, and you won't have an enemy in the place, unless it is yourself," said Jones, as they parted, showing that tendency to be didactic, which men who have made a little money so soon pick up.

Jack caught his train back to Fetchester, and as he walked through the quiet little town, it seemed to him that the two last years had passed away like a dream and left nothing behind but bitterness. The place and the people seemed just the same, he thought, as he turned into the square by the old school. The scene reminded him of his last angry interview with Nelly Paradine. How seldom he had remembered her during the last two years! And as he thought of her, a little figure came round under the elms into the square. It seemed as if his thoughts had suddenly taken visible form. It was Nelly Paradine; he had taken enough interest in her to know that she had left Fetchester, but there she was. And she came up to him with a smile of recognition in her face. She had been on her way from the house of the people to whom she had been governess, to London, when she heard the account of the trial in the paper. She had often enough thought of that last angry parting with Jack. She had accused herself and thought how unjust she had been to him. But it had seemed impossible for her to make up the quarrel when their lots in life seemed to have drifted so far apart. As she read the trial, she suddenly resolved that she would get out at Fetchester Station, see Mrs. Warleigh,—and go on by a later train. Mrs. Warleigh had seemed delighted to see her, and all the charm of their old friendship had come back. Then she had heard of Jack's engagement. She was glad, so she told herself, to hear it. The girl who stuck to Jack, caring nothing for his change of fortune, would make a good wife, and he would work for her, and they would be happy. She felt relieved that Jack was not at home, still, when she met him, there was no restraint in her manner or in her honest little face, and she shook hands with him, as if they had never been more or less than friends.

Jack walked back to the station with her to see her into her train. As they walked along they both thought of the last time they had spoken together. She at last spoke about it. " It was better that things should be as they were," she said, " but she was sorry that she had been unfair and unjust to him," and then she went on to say that she was so glad to hear of his engagement, and hoped he would be happy.

I 2

The explanation was a somewhat
awkward one, and both of them felt more
ill at ease after Jack somewhat bitterly
explained that Kate Cottingham's hand,
as well as the baronetcy and estate, had
gone with the jury's verdict; and that
she was now Lady Warleigh. Perhaps
they were both glad when the train started.

As Nelly leaned back in the carriage,
she began to blame herself, though she
hardly put her thoughts into words, and
would have been angry with herself if
she had done so, for having allowed Jack
to become the prey of such a bad girl as
Miss Cottingham had proved herself to
be.

Jack found himself thinking a good
deal about this meeting, though he was
still miserable and heart-broken. Perhaps
it was lucky that he had a counter-
irritant in his loss of fortune.

The next morning he had decided his
plans. He would follow Jones's example,
and go to the land of diamonds. He
determined on this step with very
little consideration, but as all the consideration in the world so often fails to
give us any idea of what the results of
such steps will be, he was probably not
acting over-foolishly on that account.

CHAPTER XI.

A FEW months after the jury gave their
verdict in the case of Warleigh v. Warleigh, Sir Cecil and Lady Warleigh came
back to Warleigh Park, determined to
find out how society would receive them.
At first society expressed itself somewhat
cautiously. There was nothing definitely
to be said against them. The stories
about Cecil and the Crier's Grand National were not very definite. He had
not, as a matter of fact, done anything,
and, after all, the question of what he
would have done if he had ridden, was
one on which he might well be given the
benefit of the doubt. The people in
Loamshire would have liked him better if
he had not married Kate Cottingham.
When he had taken Jack's estates and
position, and his very name away from
him, he might at least have let the girl
go whom Jack was to have married, and

whom Loamshire did not want. They were not inclined to think well of Kate, and thought that she had been unusually heartless and scheming ; but then society admitted that that was nothing against her character ; and then she was mistress of Warleigh, so after all they had to make the best of her. Cecil professed to be very much hurt at the line Jack had taken.

" I was bound to do what I did ; law is law, and if the property is mine, I ought to have it ; but I would have seen that he wanted for nothing, and had a fair chance to get on," he would say, after he had lamented his nephew's folly in going away from England, and refusing his overtures of friendship.

" Well, you can't expect him to dote on you," said Lord Bamborough, when Cecil had spoken to him on the subject. " You didn't leave him much, did you? though—" but he did not finish his sentence, for it occurred, even to him, that it would be rude to say, that in saving Jack from marrying Kate, Cecil had done him a good turn, which out-balanced the rest. " How do you find the county people ? " added his lordship, " a little standoffish, I daresay. You see they thoroughly grasp stories about six months after everybody else has forgotten them. But they'll come all right in time, though I can't understand any reasonable human being caring what they think."

But Cecil did care a good deal, and Kate cared more.

" The cant of Bohemianism is all very well for foxes who have lost their tails, or for those who can afford it, because their position is assured," she said to him, when he grumbled at the dulness of Warleigh, and suggested that they should fill the house with cheery, pleasant people, who wouldn't trouble their heads about the stories that were told of them.

" I intend you to be member for the county, and to have all these good people who look askance at us, at our feet ; only at first we must lie low."

And in time they were to some extent rewarded. One by one all the magnates of the county came to call, and Cecil, remembering what bores he had always thought them in his father's time, was surprised with himself at the pleasure the sight of their dull faces gave him. But the county people were not cordial, and they both became impatient. He agreed willingly enough to his wife's ambitions for him. He was sick of sport and racing, and intended to find a new excitement in politics, and to. show that he was fit for better things than the life of a man of pleasure ! There would soon be a vacancy in the representation of the county, and he determined in his own mind that he would be the future member.

To a certain extent he reckoned without his host. When the time drew near, Lord Bamborough, who, as he put it, always " stuck to his pals " unless they did anything to worry him personally, suggested Sir Cecil Warleigh's name at a meeting of the local leaders of the party, but he was somewhat snubbed for his pains.

" You see, old chap, they're not altogether used to you yet. That old donkey Oldlands said something about there being ugly stories of your turf transactions, while somebody else said that the poor people wouldn't like you ; they didn't like your supplanting Jack."

" I'm going to stand, though, and they'll find out their mistake," answered Cecil, " I shall go on the other side."

" I like your pluck, perhaps it's a good hedge for a gentleman to be a Radical; though I think you a fool to go into politics at all. It's not like the turf, though —a business in which you can get into trouble for going crooked. No, it's a game at which cheating is fair," answered Cecil's out-spoken young friend, who had formed opinions of his own on a variety of subjects.

Parties at that time in Loamshire were somewhat equally divided. The parties who are Conservatives elsewhere, were Conservatives there. But Lord Overbearing, who was the great land-owner in the division, is, as every one knows, a consistent and advanced Liberal. Looking down as he does on humanity from such an altitude, it is impossible for him to recognize class distinctions amongst his neighbours. There is also a large population of miners and manufacturers in one corner of the county. The accepted Radical candidate had been that great orator, Saul Budkin —Budkin, the Hedgerow Tribune—as he was called by agitators, dupes, and penny-a-liners.

But Budkin had fallen under a cloud. A semi-domestic quarrel with a lady, ending in his appearance at a police court, published to the world the fact that he was the support of a luxuriously furnished villa in St. John's Wood ; this was awkward, for Budkin's simple cottage home—the same in which he used to live when a day-labourer—and his peasant wife, with her neat homely dress, had been made immense capital of for political advertising purposes by himself and his admirers on the Radical press. He

might have got over this in time, for he
had the advantage of having the severest
moralists on his own side in politics, and
the way he denounced those who assailed
him for violating the sanctity of private
life—he had always been one of the
most scathing denouncers of aristocratic
vice—was really eloquent. Unfortunately
for him, however, this revelation as to
his mode of life caused some unkind
people to look into the accounts of a
labour organization which he managed,
and he found it best to disappear and go
under. Budkin had rather sickened the
Radicals of Loamshire, of working-men
leaders, and they were all the more
inclined to adopt an aristocratic Radical,
who, though born in the purple, was
thorough in his sympathy with the
people's cause.

Lord Overbearing expressed himself
satisfied with Cecil. He was a Pharisee
of the strictest sect, and the ugly story of
the Grand National had come to his ears.
He considered, however, that all racing
men were dishonest and immoral, an
opinion that gave him much comfort, as
so many of his brother peers raced.

"It was not worth while discussing
what a man did on the turf," he said.
"Sir Cecil Warleigh, like many another

man on the other side, and some, he regretted to say, on his, had been tainted by it, but he had reformed." So Cecil was accepted by the great Radical party, and patronized by Lord Overbearing, and though other people might not approve of them, he and Kate were fairly contented.

There was one thing which Kate cared more about even than how society would treat her, and that was, what her father would think of her. She shrank from the idea of losing his affection.

Guy Cottingham's answer to the letter she had written to him on the day she went away with Cecil had been a laconic one. He saw no use of approving or disapproving of what she had done. However, when they met again, Kate knew that she still had all the love he had always given her. "A man would be a fool to quarrel with his daughter for being a woman; I have no reason to expect her to be an angel," thought the General, who believed in the doctrine of heredity. He thought she seemed happy, and was more beautiful than ever, and she well became the grand old house of which she was the mistress. After all, things were best as they were. Cecil suited her much better than Jack.

CHAPTER XII.

A SPOILT SPEECH.

As Cecil was to be the Radical candidate, Warleigh Park was chosen for the Liberal and Radical picnic at which the party is yearly refreshed with buns, cake, tea, and surreptitious gin (for though the great temperance interest has to be conciliated, there is a type of urban Radical who will have his gin) and words of wisdom from the fifth-rate political star, who will always be willing to talk two columns to get ten lines of report. Cecil, as he looked at his guests of the upper ten, thought to himself, that if it be true that *on* the turf or *under* it all men are equal, it is also the case that politics bring an odd lot together. There was one of those curious productions of modern time, a female politician. Then there was the editor of a society paper, a gentleman who had been kicked in almost every capital in Europe, and had been the hero

of so many discreditable *fracas*, which
were public property, that the most
malicious of libellers could not find one
light spot in his reputation to throw dirt
at, and so, being safe from retaliation, he
distinguished himself as the editor of a
journal whose *raison d'être* was attacks
on private character. He had once been
quite a second-rate star as a funny man,
but, growing musty and dull as a
humorist, set up for a serious politician,
and became amusing only to those who
were brutal enough to laugh at premature
mental decay. There was a politician
with a double-barrelled name, Mr. Snub-
Receive—who was not a mediocrity—
Heaven help the residue if he were. All
these celebrities and several local stars
were given seats on a platform in
the Park. Lord Overbearing was there
of course, treating the humblest and the
most important of those present with the
same air of impertinent patronage.

Cecil Warleigh's speech was to be an
important one, and to be a public confession of his faith. He and Kate had
very carefully prepared it, and he was
thoroughly confident and satisfied with
himself ; and when the Radical lord had
hemmed and hawed through a few
entences, principally about himself, and

the editor had made a *speech*, which confused most of his listeners, for the Loamshire folk did not know of the change that had come over him, and tried to be amused—Cecil got up and began to make a good impression on his audience.

At first the politician with the double-barrelled name felt jealous and annoyed —for the lower stages of politics, like everything else, were overcrowded, and he felt a fifth-rater's jealousy at seeing another man on his own side do well. But after a sentence or two, he became reassured and more happy. Cecil began to stutter and stammer, and his glance seemed nervously fixed on a corner of the platform ; after a minute or two he got a little better, but there seemed to be some influence at work which spoiled his speech.

" He ain't 'ole souled, you don't get the heloquence out 'o 'im you got out o' Budkin," remarked a dissenting minister, who was also a prominent politician, to his neighbour.

" But then you never get nothink else out of Budkin, I am one as thinks one ought to take from, not to give to the party as wants yer vote," answered the other, who was a politician of an older school.

In the corner of the platform there sat two persons who attracted Cecil's attention, and put him out in his speech. They were not politicians, they were not local men, and they were not—and Cecil declared they never should be thought— his personal friends.

Mr. Christopher Lukes, attorney-at-law, of Burleigh Street, Strand, and Colonel Beamish. What they were doing there, Cecil did not know, but he declared he would have it out with them, and Beamish, at all events, should never trouble him again. Beamish was aggressive, and loud in applauding Cecil, as if the whole thing were an immense joke, and attracted a good deal of attention. Cecil had had a good deal to say about political morality and honesty, and any references of the sort never failed to draw Beamish. They attracted the attention of the Radical lord, who looked disgusted, but recollected that they were not much worse than any one else ; and when he came across Beamish, after the speeches were over, addressed him as " my good friend," and said that he hoped he would do all he could to win the election for the good cause.

" Oh, you've got a hot 'un for a

candidate, my good friend," answered
Beamish, who, to do him justice, did not
care a straw for any lord who was not a
steward of a race meeting, with a power
to get him warned off. "If he doesn't
win for you on the straight, he will on
the cross."

"Look here, Warleigh," said the
editor, who had a large acquaintance
with fishy characters, "get rid of those
two fellows, they know something about
you of course, or they wouldn't come
here; but mark my words, nothing they
can say will do you as much harm as
knowing them will. You'll find that
you'll have to be respectable. I don't
go in for respectability, but then my
position in the party allows me to do
what I like."

"I mean to get rid of them," said
Cecil, clenching his teeth, and looking
savage. Then he walked up to Beamish
and Lukes, who were in the garden in
front of the house.

"How do you dare to come here?" he
asked, speaking to both of them.

Beamish gave a hoarse laugh, Lukes
looked quiet and dangerous.

"I came down here with the Colonel, he
meant to have an interview with you, and
I wished to be present at it," said Lukes.

" We will get the interview over, and then you can go," said Cecil, pointing to a window which was open on to the lawn, and motioning them into the room, he followed, and then bursting into a volley of abuse, asked them why they had come there.

" I have done with both of you, infernal thieves, curse you ! " he concluded.

" No, Sir Cecil Warleigh, you have not," said Lukes quietly, "there is a large account which you can't raise the money to pay yet."

" It is charged on the estates, so you've plenty of security for your money, which you know you'll get, though it was an infernal robbery."

" I don't like the security, though. The estates are good enough, but your title isn't all it might be," answered Lukes, " when you have heard what the Colonel has to say, you will know what I mean."

Cecil noticed that Lukes paid unusual deference to Beamish, and did not at all like this.

" Yes, Sir Cecil, you had better listen to me ; you have been good enough to cut me once or twice, but I laughed in my sleeve all the time, for I knew that I could make you sing a different tune.

Just listen to this—" and Beamish told the story he had told before to Kit Lukes. When he had finished, Cecil laughed in his face.

" Do you think I am fool enough to believe that ? " he said.

" Kit believes it, you had better ask him if it's true. And just to begin with, here's a photo of me in the old days. I stuck to it because I like to see what I looked like before I broke my nose. If you remember Jack Warleigh, you'll know whether I looked like him or no."

Beamish pulled out a specimen of the early days of photography. Hideous, crude, and faded as it was, it was obviously a striking likeness. It was Beamish, Cecil felt certain, and yet it was strangely like what he remembered of his half-brother, and the pictures he had seen of him. Lukes also had to tell him that he had cautiously made inquiries which tended to confirm Beamish's story.

" Yours was a touch-and-go case before it was won. If the riding had been a bit better on the other side, they might have gone near beating us," Kit Lukes said in conclusion.

Cecil had made much the same suggestion that Kit had :—

" Who would believe Beamish ? How could he go into the box ? "

It was characteristic of Beamish, that he had made no attempt to hide the weak points in his armour. He was a criminal whom the police wanted, and would take, if they knew his identity. But that was how he played " bluff." He would, once for all, let the others see that he was not afraid of their daring to use such knowledge against him.

" I have just one more card to play, my boy. A man has always got to be somewhere. That was the case with Captain Warleigh, and it happened at that time that he was a gent I took a great interest in, and I found out where he was on that day. Now, Sir Cecil Warleigh, that is the only card I ain't going to face yet. Don't hurry about the matter ; take a week or two, look round the place and think over it, and then we'll talk about terms. And now—adieu ! unless you are going to make another speech about honesty. If you are, I'll stop and listen to it."

Beamish left the room, and Cecil had a word or two with Lukes.

On being left alone, he sat some time thinking.

" By George ! it's a plucky game, but I'll play it," he said, as he got up and threw his cigarette away.

CHAPTER XIII.

SEA AND VELDT.

WHEN he had once decided where he would go, it did not take Jack Warleigh many days to get ready; and, within two weeks after the jury had given their verdict in "Warleigh *v.* Warleigh," he was on board the *Arab*, as a second-class passenger bound for Cape Town.

"I advise you to go first class," said General Cottingham, it is pretty much in a man's choice whether he goes through the world first or second, and believe me, first is pleasantest and best. If you take my advice, you'll not go out there at all, but if you must go—go out in some sort of style, and stick to your right position."

"My position—what is it? Who am I?" Jack answered bitterly.

"Take my advice, and stick to it that you are Sir John Warleigh. I believe you are, and every good fellow who ever knew your father must believe the same thing." For all the General urged, Jack was not to be shaken from his resolve, which after all inconvenienced him very little, except that he had somewhat plainer accommodation and society than he would have had first class, and a more limited privilege on deck. But his lot was very bearable, and the change of life was not bad for him. In the early twenties, one has plenty of " rebound " in one, even if one has lost one's name and fortune, and one's lady-love has, under such a stress of circumstance, proved herself untrue. Perhaps the philosophy is wanted which in after years would teach one to think that the gain of the latest loss made up for the others. But in recovering from the hammering from Fate which Jack had undergone, philosophy would have been but a poor exchange for the elasticity of youth. When he stared into the sea of an evening, and smoked, thinking over the past life which seemed to have come so thoroughly to an end, he found himself more often thinking of Nelly Paradine's honest, thoughtful face, than he did of the woman who had treated him so cruelly. Sometimes his thoughts would go back to Kate, and he seemed to hear the sad caressing tones of the voice that used to

sound so sweetly in his ears; and he
would remember her face, and the look
that would come into those wonderful
grey eyes of hers, which, he could have
sworn, could never have come there
unless she had cared for him. Yet, all
the time, she was deceiving him. "I
wonder whether they are all the same,
confound 'em;" he would think, as he
watched a buxom English girl of the
lower class listening to the love-making
of a young blacksmith who was going to
Cape Colony. Well, no one ever bore his
punishment the easier from knowing that
it was the common lot. However, Jack
did not mope all the way out. He played
poker with some American miners, who
were going to prospect for gold in
the Transvaal, and he listened eagerly to
their talk about gold-digging and prospecting. Of all forms of money-getting,
there is none that has so little effect in
spoiling those who follow it, as looking
for gold; taking it only from Mother
Earth, who yields it with an ungrudging
hand to any one who can find it. Gold-
diggers have their faults, spending
recklessly, and making up for hard work
and privations by coarse self-indulgence;
but, as a rule, they are honest men, who
can look their fellow-man in the face,

for though on not much provocation
they will assault him dangerously or
murderously, their hands are not
accustomed to find their way to his
pockets. Diggers too are in a way
aristocrats ; for working for themselves
with no boss over them, the rest of the
human race that they have much to do
with are canteen-keepers, store-keepers,
gold-buyers and others, who exist more
or less to minister to their wants, and
who in mining camps are always looked
down upon as belonging to an inferior race.

Jack was bored with most of his other
fellow passengers. There was the
respectable young mechanic with his
Reynolds' newspaper which he brought
with him, and read till it became too
ragged and torn, and then aired its
opinions *ad nauseam*. The British lower
middle-class matron, who, rightly perhaps, assumed that a young man of Jack's
appearance, who was going second-class,
had most likely been up to something,
had in consequence looked askance at
him. That good lady's daughters, one of
whom accepted the attentions of the
young blacksmith, and was happy· and
occupied ; and the other, who after
some days found that the continuous
reading of penny novels began to pall

upon her; and by way of a change began to take great interest in Jack and to resent his want of attention to her. The father of the family, a baker, who, as they neared the tropics, began to look thoughtful, doubting in his own mind whether bread would be eaten, and bakers be wanted, in the strange land he was going to. The bright-eyed young Jew, who talked a great deal on the voyage, but never told anything about himself—what he intended to do or where he was going : though one could be pretty sure the diamond-fields was his destination. None of these interested Jack very much, but the diggers were capital fellows, and when he landed at Cape Town and left them to go round to Natal, their parting was a very effusive one.

" Look hyar, youngster, whenever you hee-ar thet Samuel Pike ez struck gold, just you throw up, then an' thar, whatever you hev' in hand, ef 'taint good, 'an come right up right away to whar I am. 'Pears te me yu air one of the sort that won't du much runnin' a store or law-office—yu air made for a digger, yu air," and after a few regrets that the " con-sti-too-tion " of their party wouldn't admit of Jack's joining them, a friendly farewell was taken.

Three weeks' voyage had done a good deal for Jack. When he went on board he felt a relief at getting away from the men he had known, and the prospect of living the rest of his life away from them was rather pleasant than otherwise.

On landing at Cape Town, however, he found himself thinking how pleasant a cheery dinner with some of the light-hearted companions he had known so many of, would be. He saw from the soldiers he passed in the streets, that a regiment in which he knew two or three men was quartered at Cape Town. He half thought of looking them up. It would be pleasant after the sea voyage to have dinner at a mess. Then he remembered that he had no dress clothes, and that it would not be consistent with the position he had taken up, of one with a grievance against society, who had determined to live entirely away from all his own associates. He found out also, that by starting in a few hours he could catch a cheap mule waggon to the dia-mond fields, from Beaufort West, which place was then the terminus of the railway, and this determined him to start at once. Still he almost himself realized that a change had come over his feelings, and that he felt a good deal less bitter about things than he had done. The world he had lived in for the last two years had been after all a very pleasant one, and it was not the fault of society at large that Cecil had behaved very badly to him, or that the jury who tried Warleigh *versus* Warleigh had found a verdict for the plaintiff.

As he sat in the billiard-room of the hotel at Cape Town, and watched some gentlemen of the Hebrew persuasion, who like himself were bound for the diamond fields, playing pyramids, he began to think that after all it was a pity he had not stayed at home. This feeling increased considerably, when, after a long uncomfortable railway journey, he arrived at Beaufort West, and found himself one of a party of about a dozen passengers who were bound for the diamond fields. They were not an inviting-looking lot. A large family occupied a good deal of the waggon. Their start seemed to be a momentous event in their history, and the mother, a peevish-looking woman with a whining voice, appeared already to take anything but a hopeful view of matters, for even before the waggon started she took such passengers as would listen to her into her confidence.

" With his diamond fields indeed—and

there—look at him, he is a nice man to take his wife and family, bless 'em, up to the diamond fields—he'll find plenty like himself there," she was saying with a look at her husband, who had, there was no denying it, attempted to fortify himself against the fatigues of the journey and his wife's tongue by a liberal supply of whisky. The good lady's neighbour, a little man, who spoke with a strong midland county accent, appeared to sympathize with her in a manner which though it was soothing perhaps, was certainly not consoling.

" Well, if you ask me what I think of these 'ere diamond fields, all I can say is, I can't see nothink in 'em. Whoy, when I lived at 'Inkley I used to have a beer-'ouse and a shop an' two cottages, an' all, for what I pays for a reg'lar 'ole of a place as I lives in at Kimberley. No! I don't see nothink in the diamond fields, 'an there's many more as ses the same."

" Do you hear that now ? this young man has been there, and knows what it's like, but bless you, you thinks that no one knows nothing about the diamond fields but yourself as never has been there, and as only heard parties talk about it when you have been making a beast of yourself at the canteen ; but what do you

care as long as you can guzzle and
drink ! "

" Well, mum, let's 'ope as we shall live to
see this 'ere Beaufort West agin, which is,
what many and many's the one as has left
it for Kimberley 'as niver done no more,"
said the little man, by way of a cheerful
remark, as the Hottentot driver cracked
his long whip and started the team of
mules off at a gallop.

" Your 'usband—you'll pardon me for
sayin' it, I 'ope—he don't look like one as
will stan' agin th' climate of ' the fields,' "
again remarked the little man, and then
he went on to talk about diamond fields
fever, the crowded state of the cemetery,
and other unpleasant features of Kimberley life.

" Whoy, looky 'ere, I've been away oop
to th' Colony for my 'ealth ; an' what's
been the matter wi' me ? Whoy, I've been
poisoned by a dead Kaffir. Oi niver
'eard tell o' sooch a thing i' moy loife,
afore. Oim a temp'rance man, and oi
droonk a deal of water from a well as
they found two dead Kaffirs in, when it
run low. They were police traps, as 'ad
sold diamonds to the I.D.B's., and they
chooked 'em in there to prevent 'em giving
evidence."

" An' a very good place to put 'em

too. I'd be glad if every well in Kimberley 'ad one of those customers at the bottom of it ; I shouldn't care if there were one or two white detectives as well to keep 'em company," said a red-faced man, whom Jack afterwards heard was a Kimberley canteen-keeper who had lost his licence. The waggon was rather empty, for the other passengers consisted of two Cape Town merchants who were going up on business, and a very important gentleman who very soon informed every one that he was travelling on Government business, and turned out to be an inspector of post offices.

"I daresay it may seem different to you, to some classes the colonies seem a paradise, but you can't think how the country disgusts me ; it is really unsuited for a gentleman to live in. We shall have to endure this charming society for almost a week," he said patronizingly to Jack, whom he honoured by appearing to consider the least objectionable of the party. And then he whiled away an hour or so by nagging at the guard for being half an hour late at starting.

CHAPTER XIV.

A CURE FOR LOW SPIRITS.

THE first three days of the journey were utterly without incident. The monotony of the long, dreary, uninteresting flats seemed endless. The little man again and again declared his inability to see "anythink" in the diamond fields, and descanted on the various drawbacks of the place. The father of the family became sober, but still received his wife's complaints with a silence that must have been terribly irritating to her; and the Government inspector talked to Jack about the social advantages he had thrown away by leaving England, where he knew quite the best set in Lower Tooting, in order to come out to serve a country that was as ungrateful to him as the Cape Colony. On the fourth day, however, Jack met with quite as much incident as he could have wished for.

The waggon had stopped at a roadside canteen, and Jack had gone in to get a bottle of beer. The beer was brought to him by a faded-looking woman, who had probably once been pretty, and who, though she lived on the veldt, in what was but little better than a desert, still fought against the ravages of time, for her thin cheeks were hollow and painted. Her hair was dyed and her dress though untidy and dirty had a certain air of decayed finery about it. That Jack was good-looking and seemed to be of better social position than any of the other passengers in the coach she at once perceived; and without wasting much time—for the coach would only be outspanned for an hour—she began a very vigorous flirtation with him. She suggested that Jack would like to drink his beer in the garden, and taking the bottle out to a seat under a thick foliaged fig-tree, she sat down beside him, and very soon began to tell him a great deal about herself and her feelings.

"Yes, it is lonely, living out on the veldt, no society, except just for an hour or two a week, when the up and down coaches stopped there—and then seldom any one she could feel any interest in. Ah!

the life was very different from what she
thought it would be, a few years ago,
when she was a foolish girl ! Then she
sighed and made eyes and hinted that
her life was unhappy, and that she had
thrown herself away on a man who could
never understand her. She was not a
pretty woman, and she was obviously a
vulgar, silly and affected one, full of all
sorts of utterly incongruous airs ; but for
some time Jack had been so bored by his
fellow-passengers that it was a relief to
talk to her. It was surprising upon
what very confidential terms they had got
before Jack had finished his bottle of
beer. As they talked there was a sound
of a heavy footstep on the path, and of
some one brushing through the branches
that overhung it.

"Ah ! that's my husband !" said the
woman, with a note of anything but joy
in her voice.

"Oh, is it?" said Jack, rather
perhaps overdoing the unconcerned of a
perfectly free conscience. The lady's
husband was an inch or so taller than
Jack, and was more heavily made. He
was a very fine, athletic-looking man ;
but there was in his face—which was
disfigured by scars—a coarse, sinister
expression. He had a sjambok, as

they call the hide whip which is used at the Cape, in his hand, which he flourished in a threatening manner as he walked up to his wife.

"You're a nice woman to be here, playing the fool; get back to your work and look after the people who want attending to. I'll look after him, and here is something to quicken you," and he held up the whip to strike at her.

"Stop that," said Jack, clenching his teeth, and seizing the man's wrist.

"Is she your wife or mine, that you interfere?" snarled the big man, with a sense of injury at having domestic arrangements meddled with by a stranger, and then, getting his hand free, struck Jack with the sjambok across the face. Jack's left fist swung out and hit him a blow between the eyes that made him stagger back.

To Jack's surprise, the man did not—as he expected—make a rush at him when he recovered himself. There was a look of malice in his eyes, and one that seemed to anticipate a coming triumph and revenge.

"So you'll fight me, will you, my young spark?—so you shall; and then when the fight is over you shall learn what a sjambok feels like."

" No, you don't fight here, Bill. If
he wants to fight, you shall fight out
in the open," said another voice : and a
young man pushed his way through the
branches of the trees. He looked about
five years older than Jack, and was a
good-looking young fellow enough, with
curling light hair and a light moustache ;
there was a look in his face, however,
which an unkind critic would put down
to dissipation, but for all that there was
something pleasant and taking in his
expression.

" Perhaps you'd like to take his place,
Mr. Teddy Brigstock, or come on when
I've done with him ? " snarled the big
man.

" No, Bill, I won't fight you, for you are
four stone too heavy for me, but I'm not
afraid of you, and you know it ; but you're
not going to have a rough-and-tumble
here among the trees, but a fair fight in
the open," answered Teddy Brigstock.

The other walked on in front, declaring
it was all the same where it was to be,
so long as he did fight.

" Look here, you've got yourself into
rather a stiff thing," said Teddy ; " that
fellow calls himself the champion of
South Africa, and he is a nasty awkward
customer to have a chance fight with.

Say you ain't going to fight a professional,
I'll back you up. We'll get off at once—
the coach is inspanned and ready to
start.

"I had one crack at him, so I think I
might as well fight," said Jack.

The last time he had a set-to was with
a bargee on the banks of the Cam, on
which occasion he was thoroughly satisfied
with the use he made of the science which
George Jackson, the excellent Cambridge
teacher, had imparted to him. With the
gloves he had been the best man of his
year.

"Well," said his friend, after he had
questioned Jack as to his knowledge of
the manly art, and learned that he was
pretty quick with his left, "you look as if
you could be a pretty hot "lead off." If
you are quick, he isn't, so keep away
from him ; he isn't a first-rate sparrer, but
he is a rattling good in-fighter—your
chance is that he isn't in over good
condition. Three other men—Kimberley
Jews of the lower type, who had come
from the fields in a cart and four—expressed high glee when they heard that
some one was going to have a turn up
with their hero, Cockney Bill. The
passengers of the coach, some of whom
had got back into it—for the mules were

inspanned—and it was about to start, climbed out again and crowded round.

" This 'ere's the sort of thing you'll see a deal of on the diamond fields," said the young man from Hinkley to the mother of the family. " If he's fond of seeing foighting and boxing, your 'usband's a-going to the roight pleace ; for my part, I don't see nothink in it. The young man's loikely enough to be killed."

" May I ask what we are waiting for ? The mules are inspanned—why don't we start ? " asked the post-office inspector of the guard, who was standing with his hands in his pockets waiting for the fight to begin.

" Can't yer see ? " asked the guard, pointing at Jack, who was taking his coat and shirt off.

" It's disgraceful—simply disgraceful —if he likes to fight, let him miss the coach," said the inspector, " I insist on our starting at once, and wasting no more time."

" What ? and lose the fight ? Not me, why, it wouldn't be fair for the passengers, if we had to wait an hour to see it through. But it won't last that time, worse luck. Bet you a dollar he don't stand up to him two rounds."

Bill did not take the trouble to take

his coat off, but, with a confident grin, walked up to Jack, and held up his fists. They sparred for a second, and then Jack led off with his left and hit him just under the eye. Bill seemed somewhat surprised, but he came on looking more savage, and made a rush at Jack, who got away. There was more sparring, which ended in Bill's closing, and Jack receiving a stunning blow on the jaw and being thrown heavily.

" Not much the worse for that, old chap. But look here, he's too good for you; have one more round just for the look of the thing and then chuck it up," said Teddy Brigstock, as he picked Jack up.

The next round Jack got two blows in before the other closed, then he was thrown; he received no punishment. After that round Bill pulled off his coat and shirt.

" Capital, keep him moving about, and you'll pump him," said Teddy Brigstock.

The next round was a long one, Jack keeping away all the time, and once getting his left in; it ended, however, by his being knocked clean off his legs. The next three or four rounds were of much the same character, Jack getting the best of the lead off, and the worst of it afterwards.

Teddy Brigstock cheered him up, and told him he was doing well enough, at the same time suggested that he should give in. "He is a good stone and a half heavier than you, and it's no disgrace being beat by a fighting man."

"I'll have another turn or two," said Jack. Then came a round in which Jack got the best of it ; but in the next one he was clean knocked off his feet. And so it dragged on, and every time Jack went down, Bill's friends gave a yell of triumph, and told Teddy to take his man away before he was killed.

Jack's face began to show more and more punishment. But Teddy Brigstock noticed that Bill was panting ominously, and that his eyes were puffing.

"By George ! You'll win after all, he'll be blind in five minutes. Keep him moving and you'll do him," said Teddy, becoming for the first time hopeful.

"It ain't a foot race, it's a fight," shouted out one of the champion's friends as Jack kept getting out of the way.

After he had got one in, Jack clenched his teeth, and vowed that they should see that it was a fight in a moment.

Bill knew how things were going, though his backers did not. It was time to cut matters short, before things got worse. Half-blind, blown and savage, his science seemed almost to have left him, and rushing like a bull at a gate, he put all the mischief he had into one right-hand blow.

The next moment Teddy Brigstock's hat went into the air, and that gentleman, who up to then had been the picture of impassiveness, executed a wild dance of triumph ; for Jack had dodged the blow, and had countered, and his fist came with a dull thud on his opponent's eye.

There was all the weight of the two men in that blow, and Jack, in it, seemed to have avenged all the humiliation and jeers of the last few minutes. It also seemed to him that all the pent-up force of the injury he had been brooding over for the last month, found relief in it. Bill went down like a shot, and when he got to the ground he stayed there.

" No, I couldn't beat him when I could see, let alone now I'm blind," he grumbled out to his friends, who tried to get him on his legs for another round.

" Young man," said the guard to the inspector of post offices, " that is the fight you wished to miss. Well, you may live to see a better, but if you do, you'll be a lucky man."

The victorious principal and second adjourned to the canteen, and over a split brandy and soda, Jack told his new friend of his not over-brilliant prospects.

"I hope to find something to do, but shan't be over-presentable for another fortnight, I fancy," he said, ruefully enough, as he caught sight of his face in a glass that was hanging on the wall.

CHAPTER XV.

" Show Sir Cecil Warleigh in," said Mr.
Adolphus Cohen to a clerk who had come
into his office in Newgate Street with a
card.

Mr. Cohen had sometimes thought of
changing his quarters to a less grim and
more fashionable quarter ; but he stayed
on in the neighbourhood of the great
prison and the celebrated Criminal Court
round which so much of his professional
life had centred.   The moral atmosphere
of the quarter was on the whole favourable to his producing that sort of effect
on his clients which he liked.

The drive to Mr. Cohen's office was an
experience which most of them would
remember.   The grim prison, that, of all
buildings of its class, looks pre-eminently
what it is, and it ought to be a very
eloquent " sermon in stone," to evil-doers,
would often enough appeal to their

imagination, and suggest the unpleasant
side of the business they had come about.
They would approach the great criminal
lawyer limp and nervous. He would
listen to their story, and in the pleasant
man-of-the-world manner which he affected, would ask them a few questions
—give them excellent advice, and send
them away soothed and reassured.

" Wonderful man, Cohen! I can
assure you, I once was in a very
awkward mess, and he pulled me through.
As soon as I saw him, by George! I felt
a new man," is a confidence which has
often been made over a fourth or fifth
whisky and potash, in a snug corner of
a club smoking-room ; and the narrator
would remember very vividly the feelings
of relief with which he left the lawyer's
sanctum.

Mr. Cohen's private room was a very
comfortable, bright-looking apartment.
It was reserved for the use of his confidential clients. When he saw persons,
as he often did, whom it might be his
duty to frighten and bully until they saw
that their only hope of safety lay in
making a clean breast of the truth, or so
much of the truth as suited Mr. Cohen's
purpose, they were shown into another
office, a sombre room, with hard-backed

horse-hair cushioned chairs, a table covered with black leather, a hard-featured engraving of a celebrated hanging judge, and a view from the windows of Newgate prison.

Cecil Warleigh did not show any of the nervousness to which Mr. Cohen was accustomed. He looked as cheery, healthy, and handsome as a man on the sunny side of forty would wish to do. So far as one could see, he was not afraid of his lawyer—some of Mr. Cohen's clients were afraid of him, and he liked them to be so—or of any one else.

"I am come about a confounded fellow who is bothering me," Cecil said, after the lawyer had indulged in a little light conversation, into which he had managed to drag the names of a good many of his noted acquaintances. "Thinks he can black-mail me."

"Then let me congratulate you on having done a very sensible thing. 'Pon my word, if you only had my experience of the amount of that sort of thing that goes on, you would almost be inclined to think that the respectable householder ought to put a certain amount of his income on one side for it; as he does for doctor's bills and travelling expenses. All sorts and conditions of men pay through the nose, until their enemy becomes their tyrant, and crushes all the moral strength out of them, and at last they come to me, and then in a very short time the tyrant becomes a convict or a skulking criminal, anxious to treat on any terms."

" Yes, I suppose you are pretty well accustomed to that sort of job, but this business of mine wants rather delicate handling. First, let me ask you a question, though. Can they open that case again, if they get hold of any fresh evidence ? "

" That is a question one can't exactly answer off-hand. It depends a good deal on what the evidence is ; but tell me all you have to tell, first of all, and then ask my opinion."

" Well, the man who is bothering me is a fellow who calls himself Colonel Beamish. He was and is on the turf, and I have been mixed up with him in a racing business, about which he might make himself unpleasant. However, that's not what he is at now. He swears he knows all about the business of Jack Warleigh's father, whom he declares was never married to Sarah Matterson."

" And *how* does he say he can prove that ? " asked Mr. Cohen, stroking his

moustache and looking into Cecil's face,
who, he began to see was not quite so
much at his ease as he pretended.

" Well, he says that he married the
woman himself ! "

" What ! that she had two alleged
husbands, and that he was the first one ? "
asked the lawyer.

" No, but that he personated Jack
Warleigh's father."

" Well, that is cool of him ! " said
Cohen, " and what do you say to that ? "

" Say ! What should I say, but that it
is an infernal lie, not but that his story is
a fairly consistent one," said Cecil, who
related to Mr. Cohen the Colonel's story.

Mr. Cohen had, all along, felt a good
many doubts about that marriage. He
had always half-suspected that some one
had personated John Warleigh, and now
when he heard the story he was inclined to
believe that Beamish had spoken the truth.

" Well," said Cecil, in conclusion, " this
fellow, it appears, did something for which
he had to leave the country—got mixed
up in some forgery or something. Kit
Lukes, who was on my side against him—
but, confound him ! seems to have gone
over to the other side—let that much out
to me, and it seems to me we could use
that against him."

"You mean to fight, then?" asked Cohen.

"I don't mean paying all I am asked. There will be no end to it. Lukes is standing in with Beamish; but if we could frighten Beamish away, Lukes wouldn't have much to go on."

Mr. Cohen looked somewhat anxiously at Cecil. Most of his clients were averse to grasp the nettle, and attack the person who was trying to extort money from them. Cecil, he thought, was bold to the verge of rashness.

"Yes, you might set the police at him, but if they prosecute him and convict him, they don't frighten him away, but keep him by you; and while he is in prison, he might take it into his head to talk—a good many of them do talk, you know."

"Yes, but that is not my notion. It occurred to me now that we might give him a fright, have him arrested, and then let him bolt again: that was my notion."

"'Pon my word," said Cohen, "I must say it is a highly original one; but do you think that the police would take part in a plot like that just to please you?"

"No, I didn't, that's why I came to you. I thought you might be able to square 'em for me."

"Sir Cecil Warleigh, let me tell you you are making a very stupid mistake. If you had taken the trouble to ask anyone about me they would have told you that I am the last man in the legal profession to be a party to trying to square the police; or to improperly set the criminal law in motion. That, and compounding a felony, are two proceedings I never countenance. I have a reputation to lose for integrity, and strict professional conduct, to which most of her Majesty's judges, have, at one time or the other, borne witness; and which I would not change for that of any man in either branch of the profession."

"'And Horner's pure Tea is the best, and—' I know all about it, and your reputation too. We'll take all that as 'read,' Mr. Cohen, and go to business. If you can't square the police, perhaps you can put me on to some one who can do the job. It occurred to me, that perhaps we had better get some one who would play the part of the police, and do the work more safely," said Cecil.

"That is a highly illegal proceeding which you so coolly suggest, Sir Cecil," answered Cohen, indignantly; and then, as his eye caught Cecil's, he stopped and laughed.

"Well, I won't trouble you with another speech. It is a business that personally I could not possibly have anything to do with ; but, if you like to have a confidential talk with a private detective, I can give you a letter to a man who is cleverer than any of the Scotland Yard men, and whom I can trust to be quite straight to any one who comes from me. But really, Sir Cecil, you are rather blunt, we shall have you coming to me next, suggesting that I should get up an *alibi*, or manufacture false evidence for you."

"Hope I shan't ever want anything of that sort," answered Cecil. "But what do you think of my plan ? "

" Your plan ! I really forget what your plan was," answered the lawyer ; "but you will find Mr. Sharp—the man I give you this letter to—extremely clever and serviceable. I have told him that I believe you wish to consult him about a delicate matter, which requires prompt action. I should advise you not to tell him more than is necessary about the matter. No need for you to go into the question of " why " you consider it advisable for him to look up Colonel Beamish's antecedents, that is I take it, what you wish to do—a perfectly proper and desirable course for you to pursue," said Mr. Cohen, with a look that told Cecil he wished to ignore the suggestion he had made.

"Clever feller that," thought Cecil,— "but too much humbug about him. What is the good of ramming all that professional integrity down one's throat? Suppose it would be dangerous for him to get out of practice, though?"

After hailing a cab, Cecil Warleigh was driven to the address of the private detective who lived over the river.

Mr. Sharp, at one time, was a very distinguished officer in Scotland Yard. He left that service for reasons upon which it is not necessary to dwell here. He was a rotund, white-haired, good-looking old gentleman. Few men are as respectable as Mr. Sharp looked. Unless he was grossly maligned, he was not of that very limited number, for nature, in respect to the way it bore witness to his character, was kinder to him than his fellow-men.

Cecil Warleigh was impressed with Mr. Sharp's air of respectability, but none the less had he perfect confidence that Mr. Cohen knew what he was about in sending him to him.

"Take a seat, Captain, take a seat," said Mr. Sharp, pointing to a hard, uncomfort-

able arm chair—the one possible looking
seat in the prim ground-floor sitting-room,
which looked into a dull little street of
small houses. " I have had the pleasure
of seeing you ride many a race, Captain
Warleigh. So Mr. Cohen sent you to me,
sir. That's a gent I knew very well. And
though I say it myself, he has a high
opinion of me for a case that wants fine
handling."

" That is just what my case wants, but
at the same time it must have bold treatment, and the man I employ must be
willing to make himself useful, and have
no fiddle-faddle nonsense about him as
not to like doing this, that, or the
other."

" I daresay we shall get on very well
with each other, Captain ; but one needn't
tell a gent of your cleverness that afore
you say what you want, I can't tell
whether or no I can do it."

" It's a simple enough thing. There is
a man who is bothering me, and I wish to
give him a bit of a fright, and have him
arrested."

" Suppose you've not heard that I've
left the force, and can't do anything in
that line ? " said Mr. Sharp, looking somewhat downcast, for he had been rather
taken with the way Cecil had opened the

negotiations, which suggested illegality and high pay.

"Precisely so, that is why I come to you. I want my man to have a fright that will send him out of the country. The very last thing I want is to have him arrested and kept in the country. Now I take it, you have gumption enough in you to manage what I want. You must make him think you are a detective with a warrant for his arrest. Take him, but let him get away again, somehow."

Mr. Sharp rubbed his fat hands together and chuckled to himself.

"A plan, Captain, I must say, that seems to do you credit. Say what you like, but there ain't no occupation going as brightens up the intellects like follerin' the turf. Book-learnin' makes men babies, leastwise that's my opinion, judgin' from one very learned party as I've had dealin's with. But, Captain, the plan you mention has one little objection to it. It is a gallus dangerous game to play for the party as carries it out, and one the Scotland Yard people would drop on pretty hard."

"Dangerous," sneered Cecil, "I suppose that looking up 'divorce cases and missing friends,' as the advertisements say, is about all you're fit for. I thought from what I heard you were a man one could come to for something a little more out of the ordinary beat."

" Now, Captain, ain't you a bit too quick ? I never said it couldn't be done, but it's a risky job, and risky jobs cost a bit more money than ordinary jobs. But who is the party ? and what's he been a doin' of, to get him into trouble ? "

" The party calls himself Colonel Beamish ; and what he did to get into trouble was done five-and-twenty years ago, when he went by the name of Flash Dick."

" Colonel Beamish—Flash Dick—why, I was looking at the Colonel a month or two ago at Sandown, and wondering why it was that I thought there was something familiar-like about him. Now you mention the names together, I remember all about him. Yes! you've come to the right man, if you want to know all about Flash Dick. There was, and is, for the matter of that, a charge against him, of being mixed up in the great bank-note forgery case. Two other men got twenty years' penal servitude, and he bolted. I was in the case, and know all about it. But he's altered a good bit. Must have had a nasty smack in the face since the old days, when he was a rare good-looking

chap. Why, there was a swell in the
army, whom he was thought to be exactly
like."

Cecil Warleigh winced at this. Warleigh *versus* Warleigh might have ended
differently if only the case had been properly got up. After all, now that he had
got the verdict, there would not be much
chance of the truth coming out, if he could
only get rid of Beamish.

" It's an awkward job personating the
detectives, but it can be done, and I don't
suppose he knows I ain't in the force now,
while at the same time, he might remember me as one of 'em, which would be
a point or two in one's favour. He's a
pretty customer, is Master Flash Dick,
and knows how to use his fists. It won't
be altogether an easy job, gettin' him to
come along quietly. All that has to be
reckoned in the cost of the job. I shall
want three men, besides myself, at least,
and men who go in for jobs like this, want
to be paid.

" Have a score of men, if you want
them, and pay them what you please,"
answered Cecil, and then they had a little
talk about money matters, the result of
which was eminently pleasing to the ex-
detective.

" Well, Captain, all I can say is, it won't

be my fault if it ain't done as neat as possible. He will know me, and I can put it to him, that if it was made comfortable, I might let him get away, and then I'll undertake if he does get away, he won't want to come back in a hurry. It is, if I may make bold to say so, Captain, a clever little plant, as does you credit. I take it that the party as mentioned my name to you, Mr. C. I mean, would have nothing to with it, though."

" He refused to know anything about it at all."

" So he would, you be bound, he is always very particular not to do nothink irregular or uncomfortable to the strict law and what he calls strict professional practice, but then when you wants anything done, he always knows who can do it for you."

" No doubt, he's a very convenient person is Mr. Cohen, and I hope he was right in telling me I could trust you," said Cecil, as he put on his hat and prepared to go.

" Sir Cecil, you can trust me to do what I am paid for. I don't say as I wouldn't for some reasons sooner have a job as was more easy, and accordin' to the law, but it ain't for a private detective to be ' too particular. If they had wanted to have the cleverest man in England on the side of the law, they should have kept me in the force. The Scotland Yard parties ain't got no one to blame but theirselves. I'll let you know when everything is ready. It will want a bit of looking up first of all, for a job like this ain't no use doin' unless it's done well."

CHAPTER XVI.

BEAMISH IS ALARMED.

WHEN Sir Cecil Warleigh had taken his departure, Mr. Sharp, looking at matters practically, came to the conclusion that he was very well satisfied with the job he had taken in hand. In talking with his patron he had insisted upon the unlawfulness of the suggested proceeding, but on thinking the matter quietly over a pipe, he came to the conclusion that there was really not much risk in it.

Colonel Beamish, *alias* Flash Dick, even if he ever found out their plot, would never go to the police to complain of having been improperly arrested, for if they only knew who he was, they would rectify matters by having him perfectly and lawfully taken into custody, and brought before the magistrate, and the regularity of such a proceeding would by no means make up to the Colonel for its extreme inconvenience. Nor was there much chance of Beamish smelling a rat if only the thing were well worked. They were old acquaintances, and Sharp was pretty confident that Beamish would remember him, and on that account would feel all the more nervous. He would have liked to have worked the matter single-handed, but he came to the conclusion that it would look a great deal more real, if there were at least two other men employed, who would play the part of police officers. It was easy enough for him to find just the sort of men for the work. He could at a very short notice lay his hands upon very curious characters, who were only too willing, for a consideration, to undertake even more irregular work than executing a sham warrant for the arrest of a prisoner. A reference to an old diary, for he had always been a methodical man, and kept a diary of his work, refreshed his memory as to the matter for which Flash Dick had since been wanted by the police. Then he commenced proceedings by learning what he could of Beamish's habits and mode of life, and he was rather pleased with what he found out. Beamish had lately taken a set of bachelor-chambers, in a side street off the Adelphi Terrace. A nice quiet place, and yet not too quiet, for there were two clubs in the street, that did not close till well on in the small hours, and any slight noise or crowd there would not attract the attention of the police. And just round the corner there was the very place where he could station his men.

That evening the housekeeper who lived on the premises met a pleasant elderly gentleman at the public-house, who was very affable to her, and professed to take great interest in the gentleman who had the second floor front chambers. He had been man-servant to the Colonel's father, and had played many a game with the Colonel when a boy. He was a rare high-spirited boy too, in those days, "up to every sort of mischief," said the ancient servitor.

"He's up to a deal of mischief still, I daresay," the old woman said, glad no doubt to talk to some one who would let her run on. "Though old enough to know better, and as might be a gran'-father, an' yet come 'ome night after night at after three in the mornin', which she'd heard him comin' up the stairs, bein' a light sleeper, an' 'aving the room above 'is. And of a mornin' she'd seen as much as a 'undred poun' bank notes on the table by his bedside, which made her put it down as he spent 'is nights in gamblin'."

The early playmate of the Colonel, none other than Mr. Sharp, paid for several glasses of gin, and satisfied himself that the housekeeper's knowledge of the Colonel's habits was sufficiently accurate to justify him in laying his plans for administering the shock to that gentleman's system which Cecil Warleigh thought would be so beneficial to him, at an early hour on the following morning, and he forthwith set out to collect his forces ; two young men, who were got up in a dress which is more suggestive of the police force than uniform, namely as plain-clothes men.

The Colonel at that period of his career was thoroughly enjoying himself. Cecil Warleigh he had begun to look upon as an almost inexhaustible gold mine. He was also enjoying the pleasant experience of a run of luck. His losses on the Grand National had been paid, and he had been received back in the circles he liked best to frequent, with the enthusiasm which is always given to the man who pays what has been looked upon as bad debts. He had ceased to figure as an owner of race-horses, but his experience in that capacity had not prevented him betting on other owners' horses, and he had won considerably. The fact that it seemed to him that Cecil Warleigh's resources would be available when he had a bad settling, caused him to speculate with a boldness that had in his case led on to fortune.

On the particular morning that Mr. Sharp had planned to give him a re- minder of old days, the Colonel was return- ing from his club in capital spirits. He had been spending the early part of the evening at a burlesque, and he was in evening dress. For the last four hours or so he had been playing, and the breast- pocket of his dress-coat bulged out with the notes which he had won. A very pleasant hearty gentleman was the Colonel, so thought the hansom cab- man who had driven him a little more than half a mile from his club, and had received a good fare.

"Good morning, Colonel, and good luck to you. 'Ope you'll have a good race to-morrow," said the cabby, as he drove off.

"Why, they all know me, quite the popular character, hang me if I ain't," Beamish said to himself, as he put his latch-key into the door. He liked that sort of homage : to be a well-known and popular sporting man, had all his life been his chief ambition. As he unlocked the door, a comfortable-looking elderly man, who had been standing at the end of the street, came up to him, and touched him upon the elbow.

"May I have a word with you, Colonel Beamish?" he said, in a pleasant soft voice.

"Word with me, what on earth do you want bothering me at this hour of the morning?" answered the Colonel, who thought that there was going to be an attempt to rob him, for he noticed the other men dodge out from behind the corner.

"It's business that is equally unpleasant at any hour of the twenty-four, I am afraid. You see, I am Inspector Sharp, of Scotland Yard, and I want to see you about a very old matter; a warrant for the arrest of Richard Walker, *alias* Flash Dick, *alias* Colonel Beamish, who has been wanted for a bank-note forgery case, any time these five-and-twenty years.

"Richard Walker, *alias* Flash Dick. What mare's nest have you discovered now? You must be drunk, or mad!" exclaimed the Colonel; but Mr. Sharp could see that he was a good deal flustered by the announcement, and he had not the slightest doubt as to his having been accurately posted as to the Colonel's antecedents.

" There will be ample time to raise the question of your identity before the magistrate ; though I may say, if I were you, I wouldn't build too much on it, for I ain't the only one as can swear to you. It is my duty to warn you that anything you may say will be used as evidence against you, and to beg you to come along quiet, resistance being no sort of use," and Mr. Sharp pointed his finger over his shoulder at the two other men.

" Come along, where to ? Do you seriously mean to tell me I am to suffer inconvenience for some tom fool's mistake you have made ? "

" I am afraid, Colonel, you'll have to suffer a deal of inconvenience, one way and another," answered Mr. Sharp pleasantly, " For the present I 'ave to ask you to come to Bow Street."

" Anyhow I may go upstairs to change my clothes," blustered the Colonel. " I may tell you that some one will have to pay for this."

" Suttenly, Colonel, suttenly," answered Sharp. " I am glad you take it quiet an' reasonable, an' so long as you don't mind me an' these two young men coming up with you, I won't make no objection to that."

Mr. Sharp began to think what he could

do, if the Colonel, for some reason, did not try to get away. On second thoughts he came to the conclusion that the best plan would be to walk with him to Bow Street.

"It's a strong case, Colonel, a very strong case. Bless you, how well I remember you?" he added, so as to stimulate action.

" Strong or weak, you'll find you have put your foot in it before it is over," answered Beamish, coolly enough, and then letting himself into the house, accompanied by Mr. Sharp and the two men, he went upstairs to his chambers.

" I shall have to see you make your toilet, Colonel," said Mr. Sharp, as he followed Beamish into the inner room, which was the bedroom. " The other two men can stop outside."

" All right, come in by all means, Sharp, my boy. So you think you know me, do you, old cock?" answered the Colonel, as he shut the door of his bedroom, and began to change his clothes, and put some more things into a black bag.

" I never forget a face, Colonel, and bless you I see many an old face I've known. Why, it was a month ago last Tuesday I saw you at Sandown. I saw you and felt sure I had seen you before, in connection with the business of the ' Yard.' "

"Ah! that seemed as if it were such a
lucky day, too, that did. I was on every
race," growled the Colonel.

Mr. Sharp's old instinct as a detective
officer made him very keen to notice that
his prisoner was beginning to make
admissions, as men will do, sometimes,
when they are arrested.

"He isn't so cool as he seems, hope he
ain't too dazed to try and bolt when I get
him in the streets," thought Sharp.

"And all the time you were twigging
me, Sharp? and yet I am a good bit
altered."

"Yes, Colonel, you are that. You ain't
as handsome a young chap as you were,
in the old days," answered Sharp, who
was standing in front of his prisoner,
with a pleasant smile on his face. "Yes,
that handsome face of yours has been a
good bit spoilt."

"You are right, Sharp. A good smack
on the nose does alter one sometimes
doesn't it?" asked Beamish, who had
changed his clothes and taken up his bag.
"Just like that, for example," and as
he spoke he let out his left, and putting
every ounce of his weight into the blow,
he caught the ex-detective full between
the eyes. Mr. Sharp had not time to
feel any satisfaction at finding his fears

dispelled as to the Colonel's not trying to get off. He went down like a log, and in a second there was a clash of glass as Beamish dashed through the window into the darkness outside.

"Well, guv'nor, that were a success, that were. He's bolted off with a vengeance. Where has he disappeared to?" asked one of Sharp's subordinates, who, alarmed at the noise, had come into the bedroom. "Glad you managed that job yourself, without our having to take any of it."

"O Lord! my nose," spluttered Sharp, "he hits like a horse kicks. It's the last job of this sort I want to be in—and me thinking he was going to come along so quiet."

The other man, who was peering out of the window, discovered that there was a ledge running along, so it was possible to get to the next house.

"Hope he's broke his neck," puffed Mr. Sharp, "an' how are we a-going to explain our being 'ere," asked one man. "Some one seems to have heard us, they are hollerin' like mad for the p'lice."

There was no doubt about it—they were, for a shrill voice which belonged to Mr. Sharp's acquaintance of the afternoon, the housekeeper, was echoing

through the streets, " Police ! murder !
thieves ! "

" Bother the woman, we had better get
away from the infernal house," said Mr.
Sharp. But the sound of a heavy foot-
fall on the stairs, told them that it was
too late to escape, and the arrival on the
scene of a policeman accompanied by the
housekeeper brought matters to a ciisis.

" Wheer's my master, wheer's my dear
master ? Why, they have murdered him
and chucked his body out 'er window.
Bless the dear old gentleman's heart,
an' there's that wicked old man as come
to me innersent and unsuspectin' as a
blessed baby, an' arst me question arter
question about him, while 'avin' a drop of
drink, an' there he stan's, while the poor
gentleman is a welterin' in 'is blood."

" Stuff and nonsense, Colonel Beamish
is all right," said Mr. Sharp to the
policeman, showing the contempt a
detective feels for a uniform man. " We
came to see him on a matter of business, and he assaults me as you see
he has, and then bolts out of the window,
there is not the slightest necessity for your
interference at all, not the slightest,"
and Mr. Sharp began to move off. The
policeman was a heavy, stupid-looking
man, who at first did not grasp the

situation in any way. He so far rose to it, however, as to insist on Mr. Sharp and the other two men coming with him to Bow Street.

" It's a werry mysterious case, and it's my opinion there is more in it than meets the eye," he said, as he stared into Sharp's battered face, " and the best thing as you can do is just to hown up as to what you've been and done with the body."

Mr. Sharp began to think if the Colonel were found smashed to a jelly on the ground below, it would be very likely necessary for him to make a clean breast of it. But when they got into the street he was reassured as to the Colonel's fate, for a gentleman who had chambers next door was talking excitedly to another policeman, and telling him he had been awakened by some one getting through his window, rushing through his chambers and making his escape by the front door. The second policeman was inclined to think the gentleman had been dreaming, as the alleged visitor had left no signs behind him. The first policeman, however, with a glimmering of intelligence, saw that the circumstance accounted for Colonel Beamish's missing body, and tended to disprove his theory that a murder had been committed. But that there was more in it than met the eye, and that the case was a mysterious one, he continued to be confident of, for without troubling himself as to the exact nature of the charge which would have to be entered against his prisoners in the sheet, he marched them off to Bow Street.

CHAPTER XVII.

BEAMISH " LAYS LOW."

" AND a nice little score I have got to
settle with somebody," said Colonel
Beamish to himself as he gained the
street after a perilous passage along a
ledge, into a bedroom through a window,
the said room being tenanted by a
gentleman who woke up suddenly and
howled out "thieves," as the Colonel
made the best of his way down the
staircase and through the front door of
his next-door neighbour.

" Old Sharp has got one for himself
that will teach him not to be so clever at
remembering faces ; but it was a near
thing. Lucky I remembered about the
window. Well, the further I get away
from this place the better. Here, cabby !
drive like mad up Drury Lane, Queen
Street, and Holborn," he said, as he
threw half-a-sovereign to the driver of

the only cab in sight, which was just by
the turning of the Strand into the
Adelphi Terrace. It was four o'clock,
and the streets were empty enough, still
he thought he could make good use of
the few minutes' start he had of his
pursuers.

"All right, guv'nor!" said the cabby,
touching his hat, and thanking his stars
he was in for a good thing. It was
nothing to him who was after the Colonel,
and the more than slight suspicions he
had as to its being the police, rather
added to than detracted from the zest he
felt in making good time across London.
Beamish, as is the custom of men of his
class who have all Mr. Wemmick's belief
in the advantages of portable property,
generally carried his available capital
upon him. He had had a good night at
cards, and in a back pocket in his
trousers he carried some five or six
hundred pounds in notes. He had a
change of clothes in the black bag, which
he had been packing while Mr. Sharp
was listening to his admissions. There
was a good horse in his cab, too, so he
thought to himself that he ought to get
away and keep away from his pursuers.

"Any one after us?" he shouted
through the trap to the driver.

"Not that I can see, guv'nor," answered the cabby, who liked the job, "and wouldn't catch us if there were. I have the best horse in London."

"Dodge in and out amongst the small streets, and keep north-west," said Beamish; old experiences coming back to him, which had taught him the advantages of taking a course which at every other turning might baffle a pursuer.

Five minutes' start in London is as good as five days, if one only keeps a cool head on one's shoulders. No one was in sight pursuing him. It was unlikely enough that they could have kept the scent and as for finding it again, he intended to let matters arrange themselves as to where he found a hiding place. The rest of the night he spent in walking about North London. There was nothing in his appearance or manner of conducting himself to excite suspicion. It was twenty to one, that none of the policemen he met on his way would take any particular notice of him, or, if they did, would connect him with the man whom he supposed Inspector Sharp would be looking for so eagerly. When the shops were opened, he was in the neighbourhood of Stoke Newington. There he bought a carpet bag and some ready-made clothes. Then he took a turn west, and after some time got into the Camden Town district. There, there are streets of small houses many of which let lodgings. "A man could live twenty years here and never come across any one he had known before," Beamish said to himself as he knocked at a house that had a bill in the window. In a few minutes he was the tenant of the parlours. There was no mystery about him. He was not like the typical absconding criminal who stays in his bedroom all day and speaks to no one, unless he is a murderer, in which case he generally shows a morbid appetite for reading the penny-a-line that is written about his crime, and for indulging in mysterious conversation on the subject. Mr. Walker was, as the landlady's husband remarked at the public-house where he celebrated the event of the "let," as open as the day.

"He has come from Melbourne, Australia," he says, "where he made a niceish lump of money, and he comes straight to Camden Town 'cause it's the part he was brought up in. 'Daresay, soon,' he says, ' I shall be the reg'lar West End swell, belong to a club and 'ave chambers in Piccadilly, but just at first, while I'm strange like, Camden Town for me.'"

"Which shows," said a public-house loafer, who, drinking at the landlady's husband's expense, was inclined to take a rosy view of humanity, "that he has an honest nature and a feeling heart."

So affable a gent was Mr. Walker, that in the afternoon, while they were partaking of something which he had sent out for "to drink good luck to the old country," for having him back in it again, he discussed the question of his personal appearance.

"He was one who liked to have a clean chin," said Mr. Walker, "that was his way when he used to live in Camden Town before, years ago."

"There's the bother of shavin'," said the husband, who had sunk into being nothing else but a landlady's husband; except, perhaps, a little of a drunkard.

"What is that to a gent who has worked an' made himself an independence?" put in the landlady, and then there was quite an argument. It ended by Mr. Walker, who was, as he said pleasantly, "one who always liked to please the ladies," cutting off his beard. That did not satisfy him, and he did some more clipping, until it ended by his having a shaven face and a pair of

mutton-chop whiskers. Then the landlady was penitent, and said, " that we all
could be good, and let those who liked be
handsome."

" Yes," said the landlady's husband,
who had got into a vein of public-house
sententiousness, in which anything like
proverbial philosophy is supposed to
excuse rudeness, " one can always alter
for the worse."

But when the police are after a man
every alteration in his appearance is for
the better, and Colonel Beamish was
satisfied with himself. In the evening
he read something in the special
Standard, which made him put his hand
to his bare chin and swear horribly.

" Warleigh shall pay for trying on this
caper with me," he said, as he threw
down the paper.

The notice that attracted his attention
was the report of a proceeding at Bow
Street. A charge against an ex-detective.
" Strange Case " was the heading of the
report, which told how James Sharp, an
ex-inspector of detectives, who appeared
in court with his face fearfully bruised,
Thomas Brown and James Jobson, were
charged with being found loitering in
No. 1, Short Street, Adelphi, with intent
to commit a felony. The policeman in

the case, stated that he found the prisoners in a set of chambers at the above address, belonging to Colonel Beamish, at two o'clock in the morning, that the Colonel was not in his chambers, but he had reason to believe had made his escape by means of a window, and a ledge communicating with the next house. The accused, Sharp, protested against being charged in that court, and said that it was a private dispute between himself and the Colonel, in which, if he chose to bring the matter into court he would show that the latter was in the wrong. The magistrate seemed to have dismissed the case, expressing his opinion that there was no ground for a criminal charge, though the circumstances were suspicious. Beamish grasped the situation. His first feeling was anger for the trouble he had been put to. Then he felt admiration for the plot to keep him quiet, which had been very nearly successful. It was all a chance that he had not kept quiet for some weeks and then sneaked out of the country, when, after all, there was no one after him. He burst into a roar of laughter. Then he sat down and thought matters over. Warleigh and he should come to terms, and the sooner the better. That very

night would be best ; there was a train
that left London at eight, which would
get there in an hour and a half. It did
not take him long to get ready to start,
and in ten minutes he was bowling away
to the station in a hansom.

"He has made me spoil my good
looks," he said to himself as he caught
sight of his face in a looking-glass inside
the hansom. The absence of his moustache and beard which helped to tone
down his broken nose, and to hide his
coarse shifty mouth was by no means an
improvement. Cecil Warleigh would
have to pay for it, and should learn that
he was not the sort of man on whom such
tricks could be played with impunity.

CHAPTER XVIII.

GENERAL COTTINGHAM IS TEMPTED.

THOUGH General Cottingham by no means considered that this is the best of all possible worlds, for the people in it constantly did things which he was inclined to think they ought not to do, he was thoroughly of opinion that it is a world to make the best of. He would sooner have not seen his old comrade's name smirched by the ugly story that the jury had held to have been proved. He was sorry for young Jack having been sent out to the ends of the earth to look for a very doubtful fortune. It was a pity, too, he thought that Kate had not behaved a little better. But it was no good crying over spilt milk. He always had liked Cecil Warleigh, and now that he was the owner of Warleigh, and a good many thousands a year, he would be out of the way of temptations to go crooked.

Kate had shown every wish to be a dutiful daughter, and she and Cecil seemed equally sincere and cordial in the invitation to him to make Warleigh his home. It was all very well being sorry that Kate hadn't shown herself a sort of heroine of romance in sticking to Jack Warleigh in his bad times, but if she had, it would only have made matters worse. He was very popular in Loamshire, and determined to spend a good deal of his time there. In London he missed Kate a good deal, so the house in Kensington was given up, and his head-quarters changed to some rooms nearer Chubland. A few days before the move, he was smoking a cigar and watching his servant —an old soldier, who had been with him for a good many years—pack up his belongings.

"What's that, Batts?" he asked, as his servant was brushing a garment, which he had taken out from the innermost recesses of a cupboard. "Ah! I see, one of the undress frock-coats that we used to wear five-and-twenty years ago. Not much good dragging that about with one all these years."

"Found it in an old box the other day, sir, and I gave it a good brush and hung it up. Reminded me of old times, when we lay at Hounslow Barracks, afore we went out to the Crimea. Ah! there ain't no regiments nowadays like ours was then."

" Yes, it does remind one of the old days—the days when Warleigh and I were youngsters together. Wonder whether I could get it on now."

" Why, of course you could, General. You've kep' your figure, and you turns out looking pretty much as you did twenty-five years ago."

Some association with old days made Cottingham take up the coat, throw off the one he was wearing, and put the other on.

" Not such a bad fit, Batts, a little tight under the arms, though."

As he passed his hand over the surface, he felt there was a handkerchief in his breast pocket, he pulled it out; with it came an envelope, "Guy Cottingham, Esq., Loyal Lancers."

He remembered the scrawled handwriting well enough as poor Warleigh's. There it must have been for years, ever since he had put it in his pocket after having first read it. Naturally enough, he read it again, and how freshly it brought back to his memory "the old days." It contained bits of gossip about

mutual friends, who, like himself, were in
London.   An account of a stay at Newmarket, where he had seen his two-year-
olds tried.   He was very confident that
one of them, Cardinal Stuart, was a
wonder.   " Poor old Jack ! " thought the
General, " It won the Ascot Cup the year
after he was killed."   Then there was a
bit of news which seemed to bring his old
friend back to him.   " I saw a Fetchester
lad spar at Nat Langham's some weeks
ago, and took a fancy to him ; he seems
a very decent respectable young fellow,
and Bower's brother, the Cambridge man,
and I, have found him the stakes to fight
Napper Clark for fifty a side.   If all is
well, we hope to see a good honest mill
next Wednesday, somewhere in the home
district."

" Bower's brother."   How well he
could remember him, coming to stay with
their Bower at York.   A youngster whose
one passion was boxing and living in the
society and witnessing the exploits of
fighting-men.   He remembered meeting
him years afterwards, a low-church parson at Bath, doted on by old ladies.

Cottingham smoked and mused over
the old days.   He never kept old letters,
that was the only one of Jack's he had in
his possession.

" By Jove, this must have been written about the time we were all going back to the other day," he said to himself, and he looked at the letter again. It was dated " Limmers, Thursday," that did not tell much. The post-mark on the envelope would supply the day of the week, it was posted June 25th. If that letter was posted on the Thursday, then the day for the fight was June 1st. And that was the date of the alleged marriage. He went into the next room, for somehow he did not fancy honest Batts looking at him, while he thought the matter out.

Yes, things looked as if he were on the verge of making a discovery, that would have turned the case of Warleigh *r.* Warleigh, and have cleared his old comrade's memory, and even now he supposed it would not be too late. It would be ruin for Cecil Warleigh, if after having been in possession of the estates he ever turned out again. He would be certain to go thoroughly to the bad, and would most likely become a regular leg. And Kate? He knew of a good many women who had been placed in the position she would be in, and he shuddered when he thought of what their lives were. It would be trying her very hard indeed —unfairly so. And after all, every one was very happy as things were. Young Jack Warleigh would get on very well in South Africa, Mrs. Warleigh did not for a second believe in the charge against her husband, and her faith saved her from feeling any humiliation. What was the good of bothering about it? The jury had found their verdict, and there was an end of it. Still, he thought he would like to know if that fight had taken place on the day. As likely as not, it had been put off, and then he need trouble himself no more about the matter. He would find that out anyhow, and he thought he would go to the British Museum; he remembered that he had heard somewhere or other, that files of all the newspapers were kept there, and see if he could find any record of a fight between a Loamshire lad and Napper Clark, on the date in question.

At the British Museum, however, he met with his first check. He could only —so the door-keeper of the newspaper room said—go in there with a " Reader's Ticket." He would let the whole thing slide and not trouble himself about it. He was turning back, when a stout gentleman dressed in very seedy clothes, with an old tall hat, worn on one side of his head, who was in point of fact Sam

Paradine, came up to him, and on seeing his difficulty, pointed out to him how he could get an order.

" Or, if you only want a reference made, it will give me no trouble to look it up for you," he added.

To do Sam justice, he was always pleased to do other people's business for them. Sam was in very low water again. Kit Lukes had not proved a very liberal paymaster, and the money he had got from him had gone. Sam had argued that things were sure to look up with him, that there was no good in hoarding the miserable sum he had received for his great discovery, so he spent it all. During those brief days of prosperity, he had renewed his wardrobe, but he had made the fatal mistake of not disposing of the old clothes ; so, when times got bad he was tempted to sell the new ones, and take to the old ones again, and his last state was worse than his first. When Cottingham said that he could not think of asking him to waste his time, Sam answered, with a humorous twinkle in his eyes, that just at present his time was not very valuable. General Cottingham rather took to him, poor beggar ; a gentleman, and evidently very hard put to it. " Poor chap," he thought, he would like to give him a job, so he suggested retaining his services to look up the fight in *Bell's Life* of the date in question, and to copy the whole of any reference there might be about it; and Sam naturally undertook the commission.

Cottingham lounged about the Museum, wondering how long it was since he was there, and then thinking that it would have been better if he had let the thing slide. Presently Sam came out with the report, the men had undoubtedly fought on the day in question. The report, however, was but a short one, as another pugilistic event, of greater importance, occupied a great deal of space in that number.

" Well, and what should he do now ? he thought. After all, the best thing would be to let affairs take their course, and not to mix himself up in the matter. It was not his business to work up and re-open a case which the law had decided. Jack Warleigh's lawyers ought to have found out what he had found out. If they had done so, Kate would never have married Cecil. It was far better that Jack should have to fight his way in the world, than that Kate should have been the wife of such a man as Cecil would become. He made up his mind that he would say no

more about it. He spent rather an unpleasant quarter of an hour, but the
matter was settled and done with, so far
as he was concerned, and it was long odds
against any one else ever finding out
what he had. The Reverend Paul Bower
was not likely to remember the date of
an event which he probably had every
reason to feel ashamed of ever having
taken any part in. The pugilistic gentry
were probably all dead, for they are not
as a rule, long-lived. And, after all,
John Warleigh might not have gone to
the fight. For all this, he was worried
and out of spirits. To find some society
pleasanter than his own he went to his
club.

As luck would have it, there was his
old friend, General Sir Philip Bayard,
G.C.B., who commanded the regiment
when he joined, and until after the
Crimea. Sir Philip was, perhaps, the one
man of whom Cottingham had never
thought cynically, the old fellow was, and
always had been, as simple as a school-boy.
All through his long service he had been
the same kindly, loyal friend. Long years
of waiting for the chance of distinguish-
ing himself, for being a poor man he had
again and again been purchased over,
had not soured him, nor had his success,

when it did come, spoilt him. He had met an old crony—a retired heavy cavalry man, who lived on the continent, and whom he had not seen for many a year— and they were talking over the Crimea and Balaclava together.

" Yes, we were neither of us chickens on that day, but I was a good many years older than you, and had never been under fire before. I remember how queer I felt. I thought of my wife and bairns, and how they would get on without me ; but I pulled myself together, and put my head on to my saddle-bag before I mounted, and asked that I should be kept in my right place, and that I should be-have like a soldier and a gentleman that day, and I was never bothered by that feeling again, for I think what I asked was listened to. Don't think you youngsters, Cottingham, had the same feeling, you rode as gaily as if you were after hounds. No man was ever followed by braver men than I was that day. Poor Warleigh, what a fine fellow he was ! wild and reckless once, but he had altered when he married, and now, by George ! the infernal lawyers have made out that he was a scoundrel. I wanted to give evidence, and say I believed it was a lie, but they said nothing I could say would be received. I was glad you could say a word or two, though it did no good. You two youngsters were such friends."

Old Bayard's talk did not agree with Cottingham that day, so he shook hands with his old chief and made the best of his way off to another club. But there it was the same story. They might by that time have forgotten all about the confounded trial, he thought; but there was a fate in it. The very sight of him seemed to set every one talking of it.

Stoker the barrister and Colonel Lyons were disputing about the case in the smoking-room.

" Hang the evidence," said the soldier, " no evidence would make me believe that Warleigh could have been such a blackguard."

" Well, if you take that line, of course it is no good arguing," answered the man of law.

CHAPTER XIX.

A CABLEGRAM.

"AFTER all," said Cottingham to himself as he left the club, " I believe one's conscience is in one's stomach, and a good dinner will put me all right."

He dined at the Epicurean, the best dining club in London, he drank a bottle of '74, and after dinner he had a bottle of their best claret. But this treatment proved a failure. The good wine seemed to bring out all that was best in him, and he began to think what a grand old boy Bayard was, and his mind wandered back to his old friend Warleigh.

"Here, waiter, bring me the *Directory*," he called, making up his mind as he spoke.

When the *Directory* was brought to him, he turned hurriedly over the pages as if he did not wish to give himself time to think.

"The Reverend Canon Bower, St. Ermin's Vicarage, Clapham," that was his man, "Chippy Bower" they used to call him.

In a few minutes he was bowling along in a hansom, over Westminster Bridge. The Reverend Canon Bower was startled at receiving General Cottingham's card at ten o'clock in the evening, and when he came into the library where his visitor had been shown, he was surprised at the hearty grip the General gave his hand.

"You remember me, don't you? When you used to come and stay with your brother at York?"

The Canon bowed and smiled, rather grimly, he had an unpleasant memory of the sort of young man he had been.

"Yes, I remember you very well."

"I have called upon you about an important matter. You remember Warleigh of the regiment, don't you?"

The Canon stared into his visitor's face. Why on earth had the man come at that hour to talk about the old days?

"Yes, I remember Warleigh," answered the Canon, and a slight look of confusion came across his face.

"And do you remember going with him on the 1st of June, 1852, to see Tom

Bates, the Loamshire Lad, fight Napper Clark ?"

"Really, General Cottingham, don't you think it rather an extraordinary proceeding to come to my house at this hour of the evening, to put a question like that to me? At least, you might have waited for some more suitable time."

"But I couldn't afford to. Listen to me. You read about Warleigh the other day, how they proved he married some woman before he married his wife. Well, the day he was supposed to have made that marriage was the day of the fight. I found it out to-day, but though Warleigh was my friend, my daughter married the man to whom the law case gives the property. He wouldn't be such a good husband or such a good man, when he is poor and ruined, as he would be as he is. So I intended to keep what I had found out to myself. But I changed my mind and I thought I would come straight here, and so put it out of my power to change it again."

The stiffness went out of the Canon's manner as the other spoke, and the kindly tone of his voice showed the sympathy he felt.

"Yes, I do remember that fight, per-

fectly well, and I am perfectly certain
that Warleigh went with me. We slept
the night before at a public-house in
Essex, and afterwards dined together at
the Blue Posts. Warleigh was never
married to any one on that day, I can
prove, and will, willingly, in a court of
law. It may cause some little scandal to
my flock, I suppose, though after all there
are worse things in the world than a
fairly fought fight. Yes, I remember
that fight, as if it were only yesterday.
Tom Bates didn't know as much as
Napper Clark, but he was a natural
fighter, and the gamest little man I ever
saw; I would like to see some of these
modern boxers stand up against him in a
sixteen-foot ring—I mean of course, if I
did not disapprove of the whole thing,"
added the Canon, feeling that his
enthusiasm had carried him a little too
far.

" He had done the right thing, but what
sort of a time would Cecil and Kate have?"
General Cottingham thought moodily,
when, after having chatted with the
Canon till the latter looked guiltily at
the clock, he was driven back to his club.
When General Cottingham got home,
he wrote out a message to Jack at Kimberley, telling him to come home at once,

as he had discovered important evidence.
He gave the telegram to Batts with a ten-
pound note to pay for it, and told him to
send it off as soon as possible. Then he
went to sleep. He had gone straight, and
the consequences weren't his look-out.
Before he woke again most likely Jack
would have learnt the facts, which once
he had intended to burthen his conscience with, as a secret.

The cablegram found Jack at Kimberley. For a month or so he had been
looking about for something to do. He
found that Jones who had advised him to
come out had gone up country. Teddy
Brigstock had introduced him to a great
many of his friends. As a rule, they
were men who, like himself, found settling
down to civil life irksome, after the excitement of the Kaffir wars that had been
going on for the previous two years.
Most of them had ideas of doing something soon ; going up to the gold fields,
then in their embryo stage ; having a try
at river-digging ; working some ground
at the Pan, or getting a billet as sub-
manager.

They were, most of them, ready to give
Jack advice, which was, to a certain extent, good, viz., not to be in a hurry to go
into anything.

Some of them took Jack's fancy very much, for they had lived adventurous lives, and were high-spirited, plucky, and generous. They were all pleased with him. Hadn't he whipped " Cockney Bill," and then he was unaffected and easy-going, and had seen a good deal of life. After all, they were not bad fellows, a too constant devotion to splits, and a tendency, on very little provocation, to engage in pugilistic encounters, with perhaps a dash too much of boastfulness in their conversation, were, with a dis-inclination to settle down to any steady occupation, the worst points of those jovial rolling-stones.

Jack got into more dangerous company when, in order to find an opening, he went among the *élite* of Kimberley society. It was true that he only had two hundred pounds, but enterprising specula-tion did not disdain even such a small amount.

Mr. Solomon Isaacs advised Jack to invest in the El Dorado Estate, a Mining Company, which owned a good many *morgen* of desert *veldt*, under which it was said there were three mines richer than Kimberley.

Let him make that investment, and at once he would get a lucrative billet under

the Company, and the fortune he wanted
would only be a matter of waiting for a
year or two. Teddy Brigstock saved him
from that.

" Ah ! wants you to put into that
swindle, does he ? Why, I prospected
that place ten years ago. It's no good,
and no one has ever found diamonds
there, except the men whom Isaacs has
sent out to look for 'em. He knows me,
does Master Ikey, and what I think of
him."

Jack laughed, for his Hebrew friend
had advised him not to have too much to
say to Teddy, saying he was no good, and
never would be worth a hundred pounds.
The same adviser kept Jack out of various
other pitfalls laid by Jew and Gentile for
the unwary, but the worst of it was, that
in the meantime Jack was spending his
money, and he began to think that it would
be almost as well to go into something
rotten as to do nothing at all but eat up his
capital. One morning, however, Teddy
Brigstock came into his room radiant with
joy.

" The war is coming off, all right," he
cried. " There has been a good deal of
talk about troubles in Basutoland for
some time, and Dick Deverell is to raise a
regiment. I have seen him, and let me

introduce myself as *Captain* Brigstock,
Deverell's Horse, at fifteen bob a day,
to Lieutenant Warleigh of the same
regiment, at ten bob. Yes, I've seen
Deverell, and I have arranged all. I told
him about you, how you fought ' Cockney
Bill,' and what you are like, and you're to
have a commission."

" But surely there are others with better
claims; men who have seen more service ?"

" Plenty, no doubt, but I flatter myself
I have claims enough for two, and anyhow, Deverell says you're just the sort of
man he wants in the corps. There are
generally such a lot of officers, whose experience of modern warfare is greater
than that of any one breathing, that it is
quite a blessing to get one who admits to
never having seen anything. It suits you
to come, eh ? "

It did suit Jack exactly, and in a few
days he received his commission as a
lieutenant in Deverell's Horse, raised to
serve the Cape Colony against the Basutos,
with whom the responsible Government
of the Cape Colony had muddled itself into
war.

It was on the first day he had put
on his uniform, and very proud he was
of it—though it was only the corduroy
uniform of a Colonial regiment—that he

got the cablegram from General Cottingham.

He answered " that until the Basutos
were disposed of, and Deverell's Horse
disbanded, he was not free to come
home."

CHAPTER XX.

A DESPERATE PLOT.

DETERMINED to have it out with Cecil
Warleigh, Beamish travelled down by the
evening train to Warleigh Station. As
he walked across the Park he saw a
light through the open window of the
smoking-room, and he took a short cut
across the lawn towards it. When he
came near he recognized the two occu-
pants of the room, Cecil and Kit Lukes.
The former was lounging in a low wicker
chair smoking a cigarette, and when
Beamish, swayed by an impulse to find
out what his enemies were talking about,
stole up to the window, he could see a
smile of languid amusement playing
round Cecil's mouth as he watched Lukes,
who, with that masterful expression in
his coarse, florid face which Beamish
knew very well, was standing in front
of the grate with his hands in his pockets,

and the tails of his coat hanging through his arms. Beamish had never seen the lawyer in evening clothes before, and he thought how mean and vulgar he looked in them.

" Well, Sir Cecil, I've enjoyed my dinner, but I didn't come down here for enjoyment, but for business, and I want to talk business," said Lukes, and he moved towards the open window to shut it.

" No, leave it alone ; there is no one about—not that I care one straw who hears us," answered Cecil.

Beamish noticed that the smile on his face was only skin deep, and that there was a worried expression in his eyes.

" Well, you know best," said Lukes ; " what I want to tell you is, that this day week the arrangements for your raising the money to pay one of my bonds will be complete."

" You will make a good haul, won't you, Mr. Lukes ; better than the best coup you ever pulled off on the Turf ? " said Cecil, blowing the smoke of his cigarette out of his mouth in rings.

" Yes, I shall do well enough, but I don't see that you need grudge me the bit I make," said the lawyer sulkily. There was something in Cecil's manner he did not understand, and it annoyed and half frightened him.

"Devil a bit do I grudge it you," answered Cecil; "it might be twice as much for all I care."

The lawyer peered at him out of his little eyes for a second or two, for he hardly grasped the meaning of what he said; then he went on, ignoring it: "Now, there is one thing, you will have to get a new lawyer—you and I both know what an old duffer Grimshaw is; now, look here, Sir Cecil, why shouldn't I manage the estates for you? I know too much about your business for any one else to be your lawyer."

"I can assure you, I have no objection," said Cecil; "the question is, what would Jack Warleigh say to it?"

"Jack Warleigh! What on earth has he got to do with your estates?"

"Nothing; only he has got a lot to do with his own estates, and, as you and I both know, these estates happen to belong to him."

"Sir Cecil Warleigh, I am a business man, and am not accustomed to joke about business, and this is dangerous joking. Suppose any one heard you?"

"They would only hear what the whole world will know to-morrow."

" What, are you going to sell us ? No, not you. You may spare yourself the trouble of fooling ; it is wasted on me. I don't care for it."

" Let's see," said Cecil, " you had a pretty big stake on it, hadn't you ? You stand to lose a good bit. What you let me have at first, and what you paid Beamish ; and Cohen's costs, are you answerable for them ? "

" Yes, you bet, he took good care about that. But what does it matter ? you don't count what you stood to lose, when you've won."

" Man alive ! I tell you you have lost every sou, except what you can get out of me, and I have got the clothes I stand up in, I suppose, and the money I have in my pocket, perhaps. No ; take it coolly, Lukes, and show yourself a good loser. You know the estates belong to Jack Warleigh, and, what is more to the point, he knows it too by this time. You see, my precious father-in-law has found out what after all we might have ex-pected some one would find out, namely, where my half-brother was on the day of this marriage."

" Your father-in-law, well, even if there's anything in it, he oughtn't to want much out of the estates, natural affection ought to go a long way to prevent him splitting."

"Well, it's too late to think of that, for he telegraphed to Jack before he told me anything about it, telling him to come home. The young ass isn't coming though ; he seems to be engaged to go and fight niggers for the Cape Colony, and won't chuck it up. If the niggers manage to finish him, I shall be all right yet, but it's long odds against that, I'm afraid. I only heard to-day, and I haven't had a very cheerful time. Your telegram, saying that you were coming to talk to me on business, cheered me up a little ; I thought I should enjoy telling you the news, and so I have," and Cecil leaned back in his chair, and, looking at the lawyer, who stood too dismayed even to swear, placidly smoked his cigarette.

"But he ain't come back from Africa yet, and unless you're a cursed fool he never will," said a voice from the window, and Beamish, whose face, shaved of its beard, neither of them recognized for a moment or two, slouched into the room. "Look here, Sir Cecil, I take it if that youngster don't come back, you come into all this again. He is going to fight the niggers, you say ; well, that means

the Basutos. I know the country and
all about 'em. Well, I've had between
three and four thou' out of you. I was
coming down on you about the trick you
played me, and going to insist on a
settlement ; but one can't have a settlement just now, it seems. So we are quits
about that ; but I want twenty thousand
if you're in possession of the estates by
next year."

"And why should you have twenty
thousand because Jack Warleigh happens
to get killed by the Basutos?" asked Cecil.

"You know 'why' well enough.
Because if I am to have the twenty
thousand he *will* get killed sure enough.
I know the country, I know what sort of
work a Kaffir war is ; and if you agree
to my terms, within four weeks from
to-day I will join the youngster's corps,
and then you bet he will get killed.
Don't I put it plain enough?"

Cecil's affectation of carelessness had
gone away from him. He was pale and
trembling at the meaning of the other's
words. He looked first at Beamish and
then at Kit Lukes, before he answered.
The lawyer said nothing, but he appeared
to have taken in Beamish's words, and to
be very anxiously watching the effect
they would have on Cecil.

"I don't know what you are driving at, and I don't want to," Cecil said at length, "and, look here, take my advice and clear out of the country, now that you can't make it worth Sharp's while to let you alone. He will probably take it into his head to arrest you. I want to have no more to say to you."

"Look here, Warleigh," said Lukes, and there was an insolent, threatening note in his voice which made Cecil determine to kick him out of the house. "I shall be just about ruined by this. It's all very well for you to put that damned, supercilious sneer on and laugh; but I'll take it out of you. You won't only lose the estates, but your reputation; I'll take care that there isn't a shred of it left. Every one shall *know*, not suspect as they do now, but *know* that you were going to pull the Crier. Every one shall hear how you knew all about this marriage all along. You will be a broken man, an outsider, whom no decent man will be seen talking to. I shall have you whining up to me to borrow half-crowns." He had no time to say any more, for Cecil had gripped him by the collar with one hand, and struck him across the face with the other; then they closed, Cecil forcing the lawyer towards the window. Beamish stood quiet, an amused spectator of the scene, as they struggled with each other as savage as wild beasts.

There was a knock at the door ; it was opened an inch or two, and a voice was heard to call " Cecil ! "

Cecil, on hearing it, let the other go, and went to the door and whispered something to the person outside, and then, without a word, left the room.

" That will be her ladyship," said Beamish, after Lukes had panted himself calm again, muttering oaths of vengeance against Cecil.

" Confound it, everybody seems to be overhearing everybody to-night."

" Well, I suppose her having a say in the matter, puts a stopper to my plan. Not that Warleigh took it over kindly."

" Do you think so ? I don't," said Lukes, " I have had business transactions with one or two ladies who came to borrow money, and my experience of the sex is, that they ain't got the inconvenient scruples when it comes to a push. Giving you twenty thou' too, if that youngster didn't happen to come back, wouldn't seem to her to be becoming an accessory before the fact to murder."

"I don't care for names, Kit, but you bet I'll earn the money," answered Beamish, and then the two waited in silence for Cecil. The lawyer felt certain he was correct in his surmise when his host returned. Cecil seemed constrained and awkward, and found it difficult to begin the conversation. He appeared rather painfully conscious of the scene which some minutes before had been interrupted by the knock at the door. Lukes came to his aid.

"It never does any good to lose one's temper when one's talking business, and that's what both of us did just now, Sir Cecil. The best thing I can do is to turn in and leave you to have a talk with Beamish. By-the-bye, if you want to write out a promissory note for him, here are some bill stamps." Then wishing the others "Good-night," he left the room.

"You've persuaded me into doing what I don't half like," said Cecil to his wife, after he had left Beamish. "Jack Warleigh was a confounded young fool, and infernally in the way, but he was kind enough to me."

"It's rather late in the day to talk about that, isn't it?" answered Kate; "and why do you talk about Jack as if he were dead ? It isn't our fault that he goes to Basutoland."

" By George ! Kate, I didn't think a woman could be so devilish bad as you are. You don't stick at trifles."

"I am pretty much what you have made me," answered Kate. " I think if it hadn't been for you, I might have been a fairly good one."

CHAPTER XXI.

DEVERELL'S HORSE.

" So you are coming with us, Warleigh ⸮ I am glad we are going to have you. But I must confess that if I knew that I had come to my own, and my own was ten thousand a year and a baronetcy, I shouldn't go to fight the foes of the Colonial Government."

" Well, Colonel, when one is in for a business of this sort one doesn't like to shirk out of it; besides, I am looking forward to the life, and to seeing what colonial soldiering is like," answered Jack Warleigh, now a lieutenant in Deverell's Horse. The scene was the South African *veldt*. To the north, in the distance, about eight miles off, were the high heaps of *debris* and the washing machines of Kimberley and Du Toits Pan, to the south a ridge of flat-topped mountains, east and west as far as the

eye could see, the flat *veldt*, green after
the summer thunder storms relieved only
by a few stunted thorn trees. In the fore-
ground a line of tents reaching down to
a vlei or small lake, in front of the
tents some two hundred men, dressed in
corduroy suits and white helmets with
red puggarees round them, armed with
short rifles, who were going through the
first stages of cavalry drill.

" Well, that's the way to look at it, my
boy, but, by George ! I don't know but
that the balance of us do not think more
about the pay than the honours and
glory of the thing. I fancy those fellows
would just as soon go . to fight the
Colonial Government as the Basutos, if
they thought there was loot to be got
out of it, and they would not have too
tough a job ; what do you say, Teddy ? "
asked Colonel Deverell appealing to
Brigstock. " Would you go soldiering if
you had ten thousand a year ? "

" Never having had ten thousand a
year, can't say, but anyhow we will have
a good time, and Warleigh will be none
the worse for having had the honour of
belonging to Deverell's Horse. We want
a real prosperous officer in the corps, for
we are so very flush of the broken-
down swell type. There's Howard and

Musgrave who have been in the cavalry. Burton of the rifles, and one or two others who have been in the line, and Jemmy Strongbow, whose regiment— 'the old corps,' as he always calls it— changes at every story he tells, till he has been in everything from the Guards to the 4th West India Regiment."

"Teddy, my boy, you will have to keep that tongue of yours quiet. I won't have any rows amongst the officers," said the Colonel. "Well, what do you think of 'em?" he asked, as he looked at the men who were being drilled.

"They're a pretty rough lot, Colonel, but they're mortal men, they'll fill a pit."

"But they'll make pretty good soldiers too, I fancy; there is some capital material, but they'll give plenty of trouble with drink and rowdyism. I should like 'em better if I was able to lock 'em up and only let 'em out when there is any fighting to be done."

If there ever was a man who could make good soldiers out of the men he was looking at, it was Dick Deverell, as he was familiarly known all over South Africa. He was the beau ideal for a commandant of a corps of irregular horse.

His history was a curious one. His
father, a general officer, and a man of
good family, had formed the impression
that the services were going to the devil
so quickly, that it was his duty to take
care that no son of his should ever go
into either of them. There was nothing
like trade nowadays, it was those rascals
of tradesmen who carried everything
before them, and his boy should share in
their harvest and become one of them.
" Business is the thing, sir, and my lad
is going to make a fortune at it. His lot
won't be kicks and few halfpence like
mine has been," the old general would
say to some brother officer at the club.
He had rather a belief in his own
business capacities, and in the end lost
most of his money and even some of his
reputation—though he was as honest as
the day—by being a director of a
company that published a fraudulent
prospectus. So Dick Deverell was sent
into a bank in London, and the bank
finding he was not doing much good in
London, sent him out to the Cape, where
they had a branch. The bank at the
Cape finding him idle and unbusiness-
like, dispensed with his services altogether.

Then he turned up at the diamond

fields, as "rolling stones" at that time always did. He was the representative of a business house in Cape Town. His business went bankrupt in a poor un-business-like way for a comparatively small sum. After that, he tried one line after another, but he never did any good, until there was a Kaffir disturbance and troops were raised. Then he found something he could stick to. He was a born soldier, and, after he had won his way up, showed himself to be a brilliant leader. He was a splendid shot, a good rider, and, despite his forty odd years, the best all-round athlete and boxer in the Colony; and in the rough-and-ready discipline of a Colonial corps, this fact added to his influence over his men. Deverell probably never prayed for "peace in our time." Certainly when there was nothing doing he grew very rusty, and found it hard to live. He never somehow did much in any of the various lines of peaceful colonial life, he tried one after another. For digging, farming, trading, or canteen-keeping, he was somehow too good a fellow to succeed. Since the end of the Zulu war, he had managed, with Teddy Brigstock for his partner, to become bankrupt in a "spec." of the latter description. The Colonial

Government had come to his rescue just
in the nick of time, by running its head
against the Basutos by a stupid and useless disarmament act. He was trans-
ferred from an impecunious hanger-on
of fortune into a dashing commandant.
Teddy Brigstock, who in the piping times
of peace had begun to develop a taste
for whisky—(in the colonies the wind is
tempered to the shorn lamb by the
mysterious way in which the man of
broken fortunes always has money,
friends, or credit enough to get drunk if
he wishes to)—blossomed out into Captain
Brigstock of Deverell's Horse; and a
very smart officer he made, as his old
partner in peace and commander in war
—Dick Deverell—knew very well.

The men they were looking at fully
merited the description of " a rough lot."
They were of various types. Some of
them, though they had denied knowing
anything about military drill, seemed to
be so thoroughly at home, that a less
experienced judge than the old soldier
who was drilling them, would not have
had much difficulty in putting them down
as deserters. Others obviously had never
had any military training, and seemed
to be hopelessly out of their element on
horseback, navvies and miners, sailors,

&c. Then there were a few old soldiers, men of good character and of just the type that were wanted. Some others had served in Zululand in the late war. There were men of education among the number, and one or two who had held the Queen's Commission. There were also specimens of the genuine home rough and loafer, who, somehow or the other, had managed to get out to the Colony, and whose loss, if the Basutos happened to get among them, would not be regretted very keenly.

"See that big fellow with a broken nose," said Brigstock, pointing to a man who seemed to be pretty well at home in his drill, "he had the good taste to be particularly anxious to serve in my company—made it a special request when he enlisted yesterday. Don't remember ever having seen him before though. I s'pose he has heard of me in Zululand or somewhere," Brigstock added complacently.

"Can't help thinking I've seen his face somewhere or the other," said the Colonel. "In the early days of 'the Fields,' I think, but I can't put a name to him."

"Seems to me, I remember him," said Jack Warleigh, "and in England."

The man they were speaking of, caught their eyes as they talked of him, and seemed to know he was the object of their conversation, and did not appear to be particularly pleased thereat.

"Ah, they're a queer lot. It takes the like of me to know the likes of them," said the Colonel. "But I daresay they will do as well as others."

. Jack and his gallant Captain went round to a tent where several officers were collected. One, Tom McDougal, who on Brigstock introducing Jack to him gave his hand a grip that made him wince with pain—was as fine a specimen of the English Africander as one could wish to see. A big, broad-shouldered man of over six feet, with a large brown beard, a face tanned by the sun till it had almost assumed a mahogany hue. He was an illustration of the mischief that native wars do the colony, for he had caught a love of roving in the Kaffir and Zulu wars which would probably prevent him from ever settling down. In fact he was spoilt for anything but a soldier. He had come down at once from the Transvaal, where he was prospecting in gold, on hearing that troops were being raised at Kimberley. Two others were, pleasant, cheery fellows,

who had once been officers in the army,
whose careers since they had left the
service, which had to a certain extent
unfitted them for colonial life, had been
chequered ones. But their adventures
and hardships had not one bit damped
their high spirits and hearty appreciation
of fun, and now, for the time being,
they had fallen on their legs again,
they were as happy as if they were
in the smoking-room of "The Rag."
Standing in the middle of the group was
a little man who might have been any
age from forty to sixty, with a large
twisted pair of gray moustachios and an
imperial, who was talking away to any
one who would listen to him.

"No, sir, I don't make much of it, any
man would have done the same no doubt,
only all I say is that many a man has
got the Victoria Cross for less. It was
when I was in New Zealand, with the
old corps, and we were attacking one of
their confounded Maori paws. Well, sir,
my company were attacking it on one
side and the rest of the force were on
the other, but the devil a bit could we
do, for there was an infernal wooden
stockade, from behind which they were
firing at us, and without artillery we
could do no good. I was determined to

take that place, though I didn't know
how to do the job, but there was no
holding me in those days, and all at once
a grand idea came to me. My sergeant
was a splendid fellow, the strongest man
I have ever seen in my life. He used to
win all the prizes at the Highland games
when we were at home. 'Donald,' I
said, coming up to him, 'put me over the
stockade.' Tears came into the honest
fellow's eyes. It seemed to him that it
was certain death, and there was no
officer in the army more beloved than I
was. But I only looked at him and he
knew I must be obeyed. I knew he
would do it and he did it. Seizing me
by the back of the coat, he hurled
me into the air as if he were putting
the stone, well over the stockade. I
can't tell you fellows all I thought as I
came down amongst a thousand of those
devils. At first they were afraid, but in
a second they were at me. I put my
back against the stockade and fought for
dear life. I fought as few men had
fought before, still they were too many
for me. At least I would die the death
of one of my name; but just then, flop
over came my subaltern, and he dashed
at 'em. Then came one of the company,
and one by one Donald put the whole

company over, and that's how we took
that paw. Ha ! Warleigh, glad to know
you," said the little man, breaking off
suddenly so as to give his audience the
impression that he thought very little of
the incident he had told them. " Heard
of your getting back your property, it
reminds me of an incident of my own
career. We are the oldest family in
England. Strongbow, the conqueror of
Ireland, you know was our ancestor,
well, once, when I had come back from
a campaign against the Indians—
with my old friend, General Dodge—we
were quartered at Halifax at the time,
and on leave I met the General in the
States—I had a little idea of my own
about fighting Indians—I put it to the
General. ' Strongbow, blank your eyes,'
he said, ' dash me if you are not the
most universal military genius I have
ever met with. Come with me, old cuss ;
together we'll whip 'em and share the
glory.' ' Never, General,' said I. ' Fred
Strongbow doesn't share the glory with
his pals, it's enough for him to share the
danger,' and we went together, by gad !
and you know how that ended ; well, but
what I was going to . say was, when I
came back from that campaign I found
that I had come into a property and
title, and really was—"

"Baron Munchausen, the title came into your family from your great grandmother, together with the family imagination," put in Teddy Brigstock.

"Teddy, my boy, you should be more careful, you really should be, for many men would not like that sort of joke. I once fought fifty-two duels in six months; that was the time I was in Paris with the poor Emperor. They may say what they like of that man, he was true as steel to his pals. Ah, if my advice had only been taken. It was not his fault that it was not, they write to me for it now. I have a letter from the Empress which I will show you fellows when you come and stay with me at the old castle in Northumberland. Ah! I shan't be able to get home this year, I'm afraid; hard too, when everything is arranged, and I shall have a dozen hunters eating their heads off in Leicestershire. Hard, isn't it?"

"Very, particularly so when their owner, only a week ago, couldn't get a hotel-keeper in Kimberley to give him any grub on credit," said Teddy.

"Ah, Teddy, you know I can take a joke; it reminds me of when I was on Von Molkte's staff"; but to follow Bill Strongbow is wearisome, though on a hot

day on the South African veldt, when
there was nothing to do, his ever-bubbling
fancy pleased an audience who listened
to him till they were tired of him, and
then strolled away.

After some time Jack found himself
alone with Strongbow, who suggested
that they should go and get a drink at a
road-side store some half mile off.

"Not a bad lot of fellows you'll find
'em," said Strongbow, as they walked
together. "Dicky Deverell is a fine
soldier; in fact, I needn't say that since
I serve under him. It's a little absurd
of course that he should command me,
but any reputation he can get for
soldiering by following my advice he is
welcome to, for he is a good fellow, and I
like him."

Arrived at the store, they found it
crowded with men of the regiment, and
as he went in Jack came up face to face
with the man he had watched and
thought he recognized when he was being
drilled.

"How are you, Sir John?" said the
man whom Jack recognized as Colonel
Beamish; "last time I saw you I think
was at Liverpool. That race put me in
a hole. I was on Blue Ruin, in fact I
had a share in her, and a deuced good

thing it was.   Ah! I little thought that day that the next time we met I should be a trooper in a colonial regiment and you'd be a subaltern.   I heard of your loss of fortune, sir, and, if you'll allow me to say it, was very sorry, there are not so many straightforward sportsmen on the Turf just now, that we can afford to lose one," and then, saluting Jack, he went away with a comrade.

"That man used to call himself Colonel Beamish when I knew him at home," Jack said to Strongbow.

"That is no more than you'll see day after day in colonial soldiering.   I am sure I don't mind owning that I started as a trooper in Zululand the other day. I who have—well, I don't like talking of myself; but to turn to your pal, I don't like his way of looking at you; seems as if he were up to something."

CHAPTER XXII.

THE DEBUT OF " DEVERELL'S HORSE."

A WEEK's march through the Free State
brought Deverell's Horse to the borders
of Basutoland ; and that time did a good
deal to improve the discipline of the men.
During that week they underwent a whole-
some process of weeding. Some of the
worst characters deserted, much to the
detriment of the citizens of the Free
State, whom they continued to vex, until
they found their way into prisons, or
departed this life by more or less violent
ends. Others were dismissed.

" Take his boots and his coat off, and
tell him to go to the devil," was Dick
Deverell's formula when a very hard
case came before him. He was rather
handicapped in keeping discipline, as he
had no power to flog, and he was march-
ing through an alien country, and not an
over-friendly one, for the sympathies of
the Free State Boers, more or less

actively expressed, were with the
Basutos. Dick Deverell, however, was as
well able to control his rough material as
man could be. For a day or two they
were encamped some dozen miles away
from the border of the Free State and
Basutoland, as there was some hitch
between the Cape Government and the
Free State authorities. The latter,
though they had allowed the men to
march through their country, were unwilling that they should march along
their border. Dick Deverell was impatient, and longing to lead his men
against the enemy, while he was worried
incessantly by the Boer on whose farm
they were encamped, who was constantly
threatening him with all the penalties
of the Free State law, for trespassing.
Jack Warleigh enjoyed his new life
very well, and was liked by his brother
officers. He had no more words with the
broken-nosed trooper and ex-owner of
race-horses, Beamish, who kept himself to himself, and had very little to do
with the other men.

" The Colonel," to give him his old race-
course title, had seen a little of soldiering, as he had seen a little of other things
before, but he felt himself old for the
work. In the breast-pocket of his cord

coat, however, he had a pocket-book,
which contained Cecil Warleigh's promissory note of twenty thousand pounds,
and when he felt that, he was encouraged
to bear the present hardships by a golden
dream of the future. At last, one afternoon, orders came that they were to
march at sun-down for a post just inside
Basutoland, where the hostile Basutos
were threatening the magistrate, native
police, and a small force of Colonial troops.

" Before this time to-morrow, my boy,
we shall have had a taste of what these
niggers are like," said Teddy Brigstock
to Jack, when he told him the news ;
" and it's my opinion that we shall find 'em
pretty tough customers. All the better
if we do, I say, for I am in no hurry to
get back to Kimberley."

Every one was in excellent spirits when
they fell in, just as the sun disappeared,
and the expectation of a fight the next
morning kept the men up through the
night march. Next morning the sun rose
on one of the fairest scenes Jack Warleigh
had ever looked upon. They had struck
the bank of the Caledon river. On the
other side rose the Basutoland mountains
with their fantastically shaped outline ;
some table-topped, some surmounted by
spear-shaped crags, with here and there

a perfect cone. The grass was green from the summer rains, and in the clear beauty of a South African early morning, the scene seemed all the more fairy-like to eyes accustomed to the long monotonous flats of Griqualand West and the Free State. Nestling amongst the lower hills, near the river bank, was the magistrate's house. Nothing at first sight could look more charming and peaceful, but shots could be heard, and as the light became stronger, they could see the blackened ruins of out-buildings that had been burnt down, while on the hill near the court-house, they could make out masses of Kaffirs, who were engaged with some white-helmeted colonial troops and some friendly natives, who were posted near the buildings.

"Looks like a land flowing with milk and honey. I'll bet there is plenty of cattle in those mountains," said Teddy Brigstock, who had a good deal of the moss-trooper's spirit in him. Luckily the river was not yet very full, and the drift was easily fordable. Teddy Brigstock and Jack's troops were the first to cross. As they came down to the drift, some Kaffirs on the hills above opened fire on them, but the shots fell harmless, though one or two bullets whistled over

their heads, most of them struck the
ground some hundred yards short of them.
It seemed harmless enough for a minute
or two. Then, suddenly, Jack Warleigh
saw Strongbow, the captain of the B
troop, who was talking to Deverell, reel
in his saddle and fall. The free-lance
who had fought all over the world—for
though he told most amazing stories, his
exercise of imagination was not caused by
the poverty of his actual experience, but
by natural exuberance—was destined to
meet his fate from a chance shot in a
petty skirmish. Jack knew instinctively
that the wound was fatal, and as a matter
of fact the poor fellow died almost before
he reached the ground. Every one
longed to be doing something after that,
and they were relieved when the Colonel,
saying, "Come on, boys! now we have
our turn!" gave them orders to
advance.

The Basutos kept in cover behind the
rocks on the hills, and sent in a brisk fire,
but no other saddle was emptied, though
bullets whistled very near them, and one
or two had narrow escapes; one man
getting a bullet through the top of his
helmet, and Deverell, who rode well
in front of his men (the Basutos on that
day got to know the figure of the big

red-bearded man on the white horse, at
which many a shot was fired) had the
shoulder cord of his patrol jacket cut
away by a bullet.　But their time was to
come, the men were dismounted, and sent
out in skirmishing parties to clear the
hills.　For some time the Basutos kept
their ground pretty well, and one or two
of them proved very stubborn customers.
There was one fellow whom the diamond
fields men thought at first was a Dutchman, but who, later on, turned out to be
a half-breed, who had got in among some
rocks, in front of the others, and from
thence made excellent shooting.　One
of Jack's troopers got a bullet through
his arm, and Jack himself had the knob
on the top of his helmet shot away.

"There he is, knock the beggar over,
some one!" shouted Teddy Brigstock, as
the Basuto craned over the rocks to get
another shot, and, as he spoke, the man
fell backward with a bullet from Beamish's
rifle through his head.

"That's a fair shot, Captain, for a man
who hasn't fired a rifle these ten years,"
said Beamish coolly, "it was about
thirty-three to one against it coming off.
And more d——d fool me, for my pains;
that chap would have done my job for
me, may be, if I'd left him alone," he

added under his breath. Others of the best Basuto marksmen were disposed of, and in about twenty minutes they began to skulk away, first by ones and twos, and then a general stampede set in towards a collection of huts on the heights above.

Then, with a cheer, Deverell's men rushed up the hill to attack, and in a few minutes the Kaffirs were to be seen bolting in all directions.

" They've got their first taste of us, and don't like it. Now, boys, have 'em out of that ! " shouted Brigstock, as one of the head-men was seen attempting to rally the flying Basutos at a " scanse," or wall of rough stones.

He was answered by a cheer, and a rattling volley was poured among the Kaffirs, followed by a brisk advance. At this they bolted with a good will, and every Basuto on the ground seemed to " get funked," and a general skedaddle ensued. Away they went, and stopped only when they had got across a small stream that ran into the Caledon river, where they had kraaled most of their cattle. They had been accustomed to Snider bullets from the men at the fort, and they probably believed themselves out of range, but the

Martini-Henry rifle with which Deverell's Horse were armed put them out of conceit, and once more they were in retreat.

The Kaffirs engaged with the men from the fort followed the example of their brethren, and the besieged and relieving forces met on the heights. Dick Deverell and Colonel Brooks, who commanded at the fort, shook hands with each other, while the men gave three cheers for Deverell's Horse. Probably there was only one man in Jack's troop who did not feel thoroughly satisfied with himself. That man was our old friend Beamish. He had been as keen as any youngster for the last half hour or so, but now the excitement was over, and there was time for a rest, he began to wonder if his job would be as easy a one as he had fancied. He had kept watch on Jack's movements, but had thought it would be better to put off what he had come out to do, for a more favourable opportunity.

"That's a well-plucked 'un, is War-leigh. He is the cove who whopped Cockney Bill. He's a gentleman, he is; and I like to have that sort for my officers," growled an old seventeenth lancer man, who rode next to Beamish in the troop.

" So he is, mate. I take a deal of
interest in that youngster, having seen
him before in England," answered
Beamish heartily. But nevertheless he
found himself feeling the pocket-book he
carried in his breast, and thinking a good
deal of Cecil Warleigh's promissory
note.

Though the horses, after the forced
march of the previous night, were very
nearly knocked up, some of Deverell's
men were sent out after the cattle and
horses, in company with some of the
loyal natives from the station. Tired as
they were, they took to the work cheerily
enough.

" We shall get hold of some of them ·
Basuto ponies, mate," said · Beamish's
friend, the " seventeenth " man.

Beamish did not answer. He was
thinking of securing a far richer prize
than a share of the price of a few horses,
cattle, and goats.

When they had crossed the stream, the
men began to scatter. Beamish got a
good way on the left, but kept up a good
pace. Every now and then some straggler
from the flying enemy would fire at the
pursuing force, but no mischief was
done.

Jack Warleigh kept well to the front

of his men. He was full of the excitement of the work, and thinking that
hunting the enemy's cattle was the finest
sport he had ever experienced. The
Kaffirs, who were driving off the herd,
still stuck to their charges, but the main
body had got some way in advance.
Every now and then, some of the better
men among the Basutos would make a
stand behind rocks, fire a volley at
their foes, and bolt again. Beamish
crouched behind a rock, to take a
breather, and watched Jack Warleigh.
He was some hundred yards distant from
him and from the rest of the troop. Behind
him were coming a body of loyal natives,
and some native police, but in a few
moments he would be hidden from
them by a dip in the hill. If he only
made as good shooting as he did at the
Basuto half-breed he had bowled over, his
twenty " thou." ought to be a certainty.
Then, on the other hand, if he made a
mess of it, he might get into trouble, and
never have another chance. He looked
at the men behind him, and the notion
crossed his mind—what a lot of them
there were ! More than twice as many as
there seemed to have been when they set
out after the cattle. Should he chance
it ? In a moment or two they would be

down the dip, and then would be his time.
Yes, he would chance it, and again he
looked back, to see if the others were out
of sight. Half of them were, but the rest
seemed creeping up somewhat cautiously.
The officer, a youngster who had only
joined the police service a day or two
before, was shouting to them to "come
up." Suddenly they closed round him,
and Beamish saw some of them seize him
by the arms and hold them out, while
others plunged their assegais through and
through his body, while more of them
rushed at the loyal natives, who dispersed
on all sides, yelling and howling with
terror. Beamish could guess what it
meant. Some of the pluckiest of the
Basutos, with the devilish cunning of
their race, had determined to have
revenge for their defeat, and had crept
up after the attacking force. He fired his
rifle at them, then, jumping up from the
rock under which he was crouching,
shouted to the other men of the Kimberley
force, who turned round and opened
fire upon the skulking enemy, who fled
with yells of triumph at the havoc their
stratagem had caused. Beamish concluded that he would wait for another
and a better opportunity, and for the next
hour he worked as hard catching cattle,

as if he did not stand to win a much bigger stake.

They secured and drove back to camp a fair lot of ponies and cattle. The Basuto drivers running away, and letting their much-valued beasts look after themselves when their pursuers came up. So ended the debut of Deverell's Horse, and one of the very few successful skirmishes, even on a small scale, which the Colonial troops ever had with the enemy in that most hapless and inglorious war.

CHAPTER XXIII.

THE FIGHT ON THE KOPGE.

A few days passed without anything notable happening, for the Basutos were far too strong to be attacked amongst the mountains. The monotony was broken by the arrival of another corps of irregulars, Bamberger's Horse. These men were raised in the Transvaal, and were a very mixed lot. Some of them very good men for the work; others, the sweepings of the towns and the camps. Among them were to be found Dutchmen, Englishmen, and coloured men. The former, as a rule, were useful in the field, though there were not many of them, but their presence helped to prevent anything like discipline being maintained in the corps. Among the English there were some very good men and some very bad ones. The coloured men were, almost all, worse than useless. Bamberger had seen a good deal of service and was celebrated all over South Africa as a leader of irregulars. Dick Deverell and he knew each other very well, but did not much like each other, though the former was too good a soldier to let his likes or his dislikes interfere with the way he did his duty.

" We shall have a bit of a fight to-day, that's one blessing," said Teddy Brigstock to Jack Warleigh, when the baggage train came in sight, " for the enemy will have a try at getting these waggons."

" But they'll have to get through us first," answered Jack, " and do you think after the lesson we taught 'em the other day, they'll care about trying that ? "

Deverell's horse were posted on the heights above the river, from the Court-house to the river beyond the waggon-drift.

" There were a good lot of 'em expecting us at the drift thirty miles down the river, the other day, and they're much stronger now," replied Teddy, " look yonder," and he pointed to a big village on a mountain upon which they could see the Kaffirs swarming down on the plain.

Teddy Brigstock was right. The Basutos had determined to cut their way through Deverell's Horse, and have a dash at the waggons. Soon, about a thousand

of them were seen coming along the flat
from the mountain, and Jack had a better
opportunity of looking at them and ad-
miring their order and discipline than he
had had on the last occasion. They came
on horseback, yelling and waving their
battle-axes, and when they reached the
slope they charged at racing pace, and
in admirable order. Deverell's men were
confident enough, however. Orders had
been given that not a shot should be fired
until they came within two hundred yards.
One troop opened fire, however, at five
hundred yards, and the others followed
suit; the result was a number of empty
saddles. This caused them to waver for
an instant, but on they came again with
their carbines slung, evidently intending
to trust to their stabbing assegais at
close quarters. A second volley at three
hundred yards made them come to an
involuntary halt, and at a third they
turned tail and bolted. As they went
away, Colonel Bamberger and two troops
of his regiment galloped up from the
drift and charged after them. The
Basutos managed, however, to get to the
hills without much loss.

"Well, Dick!" said Bamberger as he
rode back, "these niggers seem con-
foundedly cheeky, but we'll teach 'em

a lesson very soon now we've come here."

Dick Deverell stroked his beard.

" You'll find 'em a tougher job than you think, Colonel," he answered, " my men have given 'em two lessons already."

" I hope the Basutos find your fellows as great a scourge as the Free State did when they marched through. There was a dozen of your fellows waiting to be tried ; and two of 'em will be hanged, they say. A lot more the police are after," said Bamberger.

Deverell did not reply, as he thought to prolong such a conversation would not tend to promote good feeling between his men and the new arrivals.

The next morning Deverell, and as it turned out afterwards every one else, including Colonel Brooks, the officer in command of the forces, was surprised to see Bamberger's Horse saddle up, and, before any inquiry could be made as to their intentions, they were off.

" Ah, Bamberger's at his old game of cattle-lifting," said Teddy Brigstock to Jack, and he pointed out a flock of goats on the other side of the stream which ran into the Caledon, " and if he doesn't look out, he'll get into a mess."

Bamberger's men rode out in utter dis-

order, looking more like the tail of the
field at a large meet of the Pytchley, than
a body of troops, every man apparently
taking his own line, and going in the
direction that suited him best.

" It's all very well going for cattle when
you've beaten the niggers, but some hard
fighting must be done first. Look there !
by George ! Bamberger will get the
swagger taken out of him to-day," said
Teddy, as he pointed to the hills on the
left of Bamberger's men, from which a lot
of Basutos were streaming down, threatening the cattle-lifters on their rear,
while at the same time the main body
came crowding down from the hills in
front ; "we'll have to chip in here."

As he spoke Deverell gave the orders
which he expected, and sent the A and B
troops to occupy a low flat kopge, distant
about a mile away to the front, from
which they could keep up a fire at the
enemy, that turned back a large propor-
tion of them. Bamberger's men, however had seen their danger, and were
riding as hard as they could for the camp,
managing to save themselves by the skin
of their teeth. But the enemy were in
high feather at their success, and very
soon were to be seen again riding down
from their villages.

"They're going to do for us to-day, mate; we shall have some hot work," said the old " Death and Glory " man to Beamish.

" Bamberger's fooling has put the heart into 'em," Beamish thought to himself as he looked at Jack Warleigh, who stood watching the enemy, with a flushed face. After all, perhaps, the Basutos would do his job for him. The pity was that he had come too. It would be a sell if he were picked up assegaied, with Cecil's promissory note in his pocket, after that document had become valuable.

Leaving their horses under cover, the enemy came creeping on to within two hundred yards of the low Kopge, and opened a hot fire on it, but the men were well covered by the rocks. At the same time a large body of Basutos charged across the flat, at the camp, but they thus exposed themselves to the remaining companies of Deverell's Horse, who occupied a Kopge about half a mile to the rear of the A troop. They were met by two tremendous volleys which knocked over a good many of them, and made the rest retire pretty quickly.

In about twenty minutes they came sneaking round to the other side of the camp, where Bamberger's men came out and showed that they were made of good stuff enough, though discipline was not their strong point; and again the Basutos retired, but they rallied enough to threaten the camp and make the position of the A troop anything but a pleasant one.

At this time, across the river, on the Free State side, there was a reinforcement of some two hundred burghers. Most of these had come unwillingly to the war. Their commandant, an ancient Dutchman, had brought them up to the front at the rate of about four miles a day, and was by no means filled with martial ardour at finding himself in time to see some fighting. In fact he gave his men orders not to cross the river, and took up a position of masterly inactivity, from which even Colonel Bamberger— who occupied a space of ten minutes in expressing his opinion in a harangue, which showed a fine knowledge of the unwritten part of the Dutch language — was unable to rouse them.

" Alla matig Kerl; it is the sabbath, and I am not going to have it said of me in Colesberg, that I break the Sabbath as you verdomde English do," answered the old dopper, who had no stomach for fighting on any day in the week, particularly in what he considered was the Englishman's quarrel.

In the meantime, Jack Warleigh and the A troop were finding themselves in an uncommonly warm place, and Deverell, seeing their position, sent them an order to retire, which they began to carry out. But by the time they had got to their horses, which were behind the Kopge, the enemy were on the rise, and pouring a sharp fire upon them from barely a hundred yards. It was no good thinking of retiring then, and Teddy Brigstock gave the order to charge. Almost as soon as he gave the command, he staggered and fell, shot through the body. There was no time for regrets. Jack Warleigh ran in front of the men, across the flat-topped Kopge, and in a few seconds they were charging straight into the smoke of the enemy's rifles, using their revolvers with certain effect.

Jack, in front of his men, fired every chamber of his revolver, killing Basutos with two of his shots, and then he caught one man by the throat, and smashing him across the face with his empty revolver, hurled him down the side of the Kopge.

It was about as good a chance as he was likely to get, Beamish thought, and he fired his revolver at Jack, but missed him, the bullet killing a Basuto who was making a stab at him with an assegai. Again the A troop was in its old position, but they were without their brave captain.

Jack and most of the men began to feel anxious as to the result.

The enemy soon rallied, and, reinforced by other Basutos, who had been held in reserve, came again to the attack. Another order came to retire, but this time they had not crossed the Kopge before the Basutos were on the rise, firing into them. Several fell, and Jack Warleigh, rather than expose his men to a disastrous fire, and perhaps to a rush from the Basutos, gave the order to charge back. As he did so, he saw a helmet, under which was a broken-nosed face, rise from a hole half-way across the Kopge. It was Beamish, who had fallen as he ran across the Kopge. He would have been wiser to have remained where he was, for some of the Basutos saw and rushed towards him with uplifted assegais. Jack ran as if he were at Fenner's, running the hundred yards, and got up in time to knock over a Basuto, with a shot from his revolver, who had got up to

Beamish before he could get out of the
hole, the latter being half dazed by his
fall. Then other Basutos rushed at
Jack, but another shot did for one of
them, and a second was accounted for by
Beamish ; and the rest of Jack's troop
coming up, the remaining Basutos cleared
out. After this the men became mixed
up with the Kaffirs again, one or two of
them being assegaied, but the troop
fought their way to their old position,
doing great execution with their revolvers. Once more an order came
to retire, and again the enemy made a
rush on to the Kopge, and were too quick
to let the troopers get away. Thinned
though the troop was from the men who
had fallen, and those who had been sent
back with the wounded, there was only
one thing to be done, and Jack led his
men at them again. With a cheer they
rushed at the enemy, who had already
suffered so much in the previous charges,
that they had begun to show symptoms of
" funk."

Jack Warleigh was so well to the front
in that last charge, that for a few seconds
it looked as if his history was about to
come to an untimely end.

Beamish and the ex-lancer were close
after him, but the Basutos closed round

Jack, and he could never make out how it was that he escaped their assegais.

Beamish smashed a Kaffir across the head with the butt of his rifle, and the ex-lancer shot two others, and with a rush the gallant A troop fought their way back again.

No one did better work than Beamish, who hit his man at nearly every discharge from his rifle, which he emptied again and again. Still things looked awkward, for the Basutos were stronger in numbers, and better armed for man-to-man fighting, their stabbing assegais being difficult to parry, and even the revolver barely brought the balance even. But they were disheartened by the punishment they had received in the last two charges ; and, giving way all round, they turned tail just when affairs began to look most critical, and Deverell's Horse once more regained their old position.

After that last charge the enemy determined to let matters rest for the present, as their main body was retiring to the villages.

As the A troop, minus some dozen men killed and wounded, with an escort that had been sent down for the latter, rode back past the other troops of Deverell's Horse, they were greeted with

hearty cheers, and Jack Warleigh felt
proud of himself and the men he had had
the honour of leading.　But his and most
of his men's thoughts soon turned to the
fate of the brave young fellow who had
led them out so cheerily at the onset.

"How did it fare with Teddy Brigstock?"　Very great was their satisfaction when they found it was not as bad
with him as they feared.　"Seriously
wounded, but not dangerously," was the
verdict of the doctor.

Though he was sorry enough for the
fate of the other brave fellows of his
company, who had been killed that day,
Jack Warleigh was in capital spirits on
the evening after the fight on Deverell's
Horse Kopge;　a fight which, though
only an obscure skirmish in a disastrous
and insignificant war, is not likely to be
forgotten by any one who witnessed or
took part in it.

CHAPTER XXIV.

ON SPECIAL DUTY.

ON parade, the morning after the fight, Deverell made a speech to the A troop, and then called Jack Warleigh aside.

"I have got something for you to do, Warleigh. I want to send some one across to the Moori River Station to see how things are going on there, and have a talk to the magistrate. News has come in that things are going rather hardly with them. It is my opinion that we haven't a man to spare, though between you and me, I shouldn't so much mind them having Bamberger's, and they are welcome to those d——d burghers who haven't crossed yet, though the Sunday is over. But though I'm in command of the garrison—for Brooks is down with fever—I don't believe Bamberger would go if I told him to ; and the burghers couldn't do any good. Now

I want to send some one who can explain the situation, and bring me intelligence exactly how affairs stand. I have a Hottentot fellow,. an old Cape Corps man, who will show you the way, and perhaps you had better take another man. You'll have to keep a sharp look-out, for the Basutos are all round the place, and your way is right through their country. Choose the best man you can, and then come round to me for the letter to the office at Moori River. You must be off at sundown."

There was not overmuch response when Jack Warleigh asked for a man to go with him, for it was not a taking duty. Just the man he wanted, however, offered his services, it was his old acquaintance the broken-nosed trooper who had fought so well the day before.

"I know the country too, for I was in the war between the Basutos and the Free State, so if the other man doesn't like the job we can do without him," he said, after Jack had agreed to take him.

Beamish found occasion during the day to have a talk with the Hottentot who was to guide them. The latter was a very favourable type of his race, and showed no fear at what was undoubtedly a dangerous expedition. Beamish, making a shot at the fellow's weak spot, suggested that they should slip across the drift, which was easily forded, to a Dutchman's waggon and have a drink of Cape smoke.

At sundown, Jack Warleigh and the other two started out for their long night's ride. Beamish at first was silent, but the Hottentot showed an inclination to talk a good deal.

"He doesn't mean any impertinence, sir, it's a way these 'totties' have. Let them jabber, and they keep in a good temper; shut 'em up, and they get sulky and ain't no good," said Beamish to Jack who began to gaze at the guide somewhat doubtfully.

For the first two hours after crossing the drift, their ride was on Free State Territory.

"Let me get down and take a liquor, *baas*. Ain't well, *baas*, and want a liquor," said the Hottentot as they passed a roadside store after the first hour's ride. Jack ordered the man to ride on and hold his tongue, and began to feel more mistrustful of him.

"That's the worst of those 'totties. They're such devils for drink," remarked Beamish, "it's best never to let them taste it."

For all that, he found an opportunity for slipping a flask into the guide's hand. After that the fellow became less talkative, going back and amusing himself very affectionately with the flask.

"It was Moori Cape smoke," he said to himself, "beine sterk," better than he had ever drunk before. It did not make him wild or garrulous, but he lagged behind and finished the contents of the flask.

"Where's the nigger?" asked Jack Warleigh, who had been riding on and looking into the wonderful starlit heavens, and half dreaming of far-off people and events, that seemed as if they had happened in another world. He was thinking that, after all, the incidents that had pained him so much at the time of their occurrence were all for the best. He winced still, when he thought of Kate Cottingham. "She was Kate Warleigh, by George! not Kate Cottingham," he said to himself, "but it was well to have found her out in time."

His South African trip would be pleasant enough to look back to, if he ever got home. It had been a pretty near thing with him though, once or twice.

Cecil's chances of coming into the estates, after all, had looked rather rosy more than once. "Poor old Cecil!" once he had thought him the best fellow in the world.

"Darn his skin! if he ain't all wrong. Look at him," said Beamish, and he pointed back.

The Hottentot's horse had come to a standstill, and its rider sat all in a heap leaning over the pommel of his saddle. As they looked at him, he rolled off and lay like a log on the ground.

"A darned fine guide we've got. It's a good job I know the way to the Moori River Station, if you mean going on, and not turning back and telling the Colonel its 'no go.' He had some liquor on him, curse him, and is dead drunk."

Jack Warleigh bit his lip in vexation.

To ride back and tell the Colonel his mission had turned out a failure owing to his not looking after the guide, would never do.

"I'll bet I can find my way all right. It's away back in the sixties, since I traded in the country, and I done a deal since then; been a swell at home, and an owner of racehorses, but I remember the old days when one-eyed Burke and I traded with these niggers, and I can find my way to Moori River."

If Beamish, who seemed a brave fellow, as keen and high-spirited as a boy, would chance it, he would. Beamish would

have nothing to lose by riding back,
while he himself would be blamed for
having failed, Jack thought; and he
thanked Beamish, and said he would take
his advice.

"Let the beggar stay where he is.
Lucky for him we hadn't crossed the
river," said Beamish, as they quickened
their pace towards the drift where they
were to cross again into Basuto-land.
In another hour they were riding over
a mountainous pass. In the moon-light,
the scene was wild and eerie-looking
enough. The fantastically shaped mountains in front of them seemed to tremble
in the star-light, and the rocks among
which their path wound cast shadows
which seemed full of lurking Kaffirs.
The sense that they were in an enemy's
country began to creep over Jack.

Beamish talked incessantly. He was
strangely confidential about old days, and,
to Jack's surprise, told him the story of
the Grand National.

"Yes, we had got it up for you pretty
thick, and if it hadn't been for that brute
breaking Cecil's legs, we'd have landed a
rare stake."

Jack listened and wondered at the
other telling him so much. He had
heard rumours, and had suspicions about

Cecil before, and now that he no longer trusted his uncle's honour he was inclined to believe what Beamish told him.

" Yes, that makes you prick your ears up, Sir John Warleigh, and if it is a satisfaction for you to know it, I for one don't grudge it you," said Beamish to himself as he reined in his horse and dropped behind.

They had come to the summit of the pass, and the bridle road which they followed ran under a ridge of rock, and an ugly-looking path it was ; for below them the road sloped downward for some two hundred feet to what seemed from the tree-tops he could see below, to be a sheer precipice. Beamish looked back and calculated how long it would take him to gallop back to the drift and get into safety again. He began to feel nervous, and fancied two or three yelling Basutos armed with assegais springing from behind each rock. He was sick of fighting Kaffirs, it was all very well when his blood was up, as it had been the day before, but riding in their country at night amongst those infernal rocks, made him feel queer and remember his sins and his years. He had got his chance, and he would do the job he came out for, and

get back to England again. He unslung
his rifle, and as he did so Jack Warleigh
reined in his horse and proceeded to light
a pipe.

"Sir Cecil Warleigh's I.O.U. is worth
nineteen thousand nine hundred and
ninety-nine pounds nineteen shillings,"
muttered Beamish to himself through his
clenched teeth as he took a steady aim
at Jack's head and pulled the trigger—
"and the odd bob," he added.

Just at that moment Jack Warleigh
turned his head round to speak to
Beamish, and saw to his horror the
moonshine glinting along the barrel of
Beamish's rifle which was aimed directly
at him. Then came a flash, and then—
blankness.

"Dead as a hammer," hissed Beamish
between his teeth, as Jack's body rolled
from the saddle down the incline, and
disappeared over the precipitous ledge
below.

"Curse the row!" thought he, as the
rocks re-echoed the report again and
again, "it will bring those infernal niggers
on me. So, he thought, would Jack's
horse, which was now galloping down the
pass. How lonely the place was; lonely,
only there were plenty of those black devils
near if he only knew! His own horse

plunged and reared, trembling as if it knew what its master had done, and both horse and man seemed mutually glad when Beamish turned and rode back down the pass again.

Beamish spurred on, and did the distance back that had taken them two hours in not much more than half that. time.

"Thank the Lord, I am out of the cursed place," he said with a shiver, as he rode through the drift. Once across, he off-saddled and rested for an hour or so. Then he rode on past where the Hottentot still lay in a drunken sleep. As he passed, he got off, and, searching in the man's pockets, found and secured the flask he had given him, and threw it against a boulder, where it broke into a thousand fragments. Then he rode on again until he came to the camp on the Caledon River.

Dick Deverell was awakened from his sleep to hear a story which caused him some bitter self-reproach. The trooper he had sent on special duty with Jack reported that Lieutenant Warleigh and himself had been attacked by Basutos, that Warleigh was killed, and that he himself barely managed to escape.

At daybreak next morning a waggon was toiling painfully and slowly along a road below the mountain path on which Jack Warleigh was shot. It was to outspan at a spot where a stream that ran down from the mountain would enable the owner to make the needed cup of morning coffee, and the boys who attended the oxen looked longingly forward towards the break in the hills down which the watercourse came, while the Dutchman and his wife, the owners and occupiers of the waggon, snored a duet. The stream was a little deeper some few hundred yards below the spot where it first met the trail, and the two Kaffirs disputed noisily together as to where they should outspan. The chances were against the one who was for going on further having his way, but it happened that he was the master spirit; so the waggon crept on till they came to the place he had chosen in his mind's eye. Then the oxen were brought to a standstill and the Dutchman woke up, and looking more dirty and unwholesome than usual in the gray morning light, got out from the inner recesses of the waggon, followed by his fat, shapeless old wife, and began to superintend the outspanning of the oxen.

"Ah! what a long time those schellums

of Kaffirs take getting the water !" scolded
the woman in a querulous voice, after the
baas had been away a minute or two
at the spring. "What is the matter
with them? What can they be calling
about?" she added, as she heard them
shouting for the baas to come to the
stream.

"Baas! baas! come here. Here is a
dead man — a dead Englishman!" shouted
one of the Kaffirs.

"What do I care?" said the Dutchman,
"I would not walk twenty yards to see
one. Dead Englishmen will be a common
sight soon, for we Africanders are going
to shoot them all—at least all the grown
ones, the children we will teach only to
speak Dutch."

"Ah, master, but what you say is true,"
grunted the old woman, "but if there is
a dead Englishman, I would like to have
a look at him. It has been a long weary
trek, and one does not like to miss a
sight," and very cautiously, as one leaving
her accustomed sphere, the old woman
climbed off the waggon and waddled
across the *veldt* to the brushwood and
undergrowth by the stream.

"Come, master, and see the fool of an
Englishman. He has fallen down from
above there," said the woman, pointing to

the ledge above them, " so it seems, one can see that by the way he lies."

Her lord and master responded only by shouting to the Kaffirs, "Now, then, make haste and make the coffee;" and then he supplemented that request by saying, " Yes, it is easy to see he has fallen. But he did not get that in his fall," and, without showing much reverence for the dead body, pushed back with his *sjambok* the locks of hair which lay matted over the brow, disclosing a wound which furrowed the flesh of the forehead and stretched half across it.

The fat old woman, although she had that horror of getting wet, which is characteristic of those who never wash, managed to waddle across the stream, so as to have a good look at the sight. As she stared into the pale face disfigured by the ghastly wound, which seemed to run round from the back of the head, she suddenly exclaimed,—

"Man, but I think he is not dead!" and she put her hand under the cord coat and felt the region of the heart.

Her husband pointed to the wound in the forehead, and laughed derisively, saying, " I wish every *verdomde* Englishman in Africa was as dead as he is."

" But he is alive, I tell you. His heart just beats," insisted the old woman.

" Well, it is of no matter, he won't be alive much longer," replied the Dutchman, " and we cannot wait to see whether he lives or dies. We must make haste with our load of ammunition and guns, or maybe the Basutos will have beaten the Englishmen, and will not want them. Ha, ha ! You think him a *mooi kerl*," he added, with a flash of jealousy which was grimly grotesque, " but he won't look so nice in a day or two."

" Man ! he is alive, and—see, look at him, he has a fine skin and soft hands ; and look at the *mooi* ring on his finger. If we took him up, we might perhaps make more by him than by the guns and powder."

" No, he has no money, and no friends, I am sure. He is one of those Deverell's Horse, and they are men the world would be well rid of. No ones goes to fight unless they want money."

" But I will have him in the waggon. If we leave him here to die, I shall see his face when I sleep, and I shall be frightened," pleaded the woman. She continued her protestations that he must not be left, until her husband—who loved peace and quiet—let her have her way.

" He will be dead soon, anyway, and
then we shall have to bury him, and that
will be the end," her husband said, as he
helped to lift the wounded man—who was
of course none other than Jack Warleigh
—into the waggon. " It will be a strange
thing to have a sick Englishman in the
waggon, when we get to the chief's
kraal," grumbled the Dutchman.

" Well, we can give him up, may be
the Basutos will buy him from us," answered the old woman, who generally
managed to get her way.

A further examination showed them
that the wound on the forehead was but a
superficial one. Jack must instinctively
have turned and ducked when he saw the
flash ; the bullet had grazed the back of
his head and taken a forward direction
beneath the skin, and broken its way
through above the frontal bone.

The Dutchman proved to be wrong in
his expectations of having to bury Jack,
for in the course of a day or two he began
to evince decided symptoms of vigorous
vitality, and to talk nonsense so incessantly, that the Dutchman devoutly
wished he had left him on the *veldt*. But
the old woman had taken a strong fancy
to Jack, a fancy which she encouraged
all the more as she saw it annoyed her

husband. She nursed her patient through an attack of brain-fever, followed by a long period of stupor and dulness, which lasted for weeks after the waggon had arrived at the chief's kraal. When he got stronger, he was weak-headed and childish, not appearing to remember anything about his past, and being happy enough employed in fetching water or doing other work about the waggon.

Deverell never made any attempt to find Jack's body, for on the next occasion they had a fight, the enemy appeared in much stronger force, and the Colonial troops got rather the worst of it, and from that time had to act on the defensive.

One day, not long after he had reported Jack's death, Beamish was one of a body of men engaged in a rather severe skirmish, at the finish of which he was reported "missing." It was supposed that he had fallen into the hands of the enemy, and he was regretted as a man who had fought well, and in a short time was forgotten, for the Basutos kept Deverell's Horse fully occupied, and gave them plenty to think about.

CHAPTER XXV.

A FAMILY RÉUNION.

It was one of the first bright warm days of Spring, a day when cheap swells came out in suits of clothes which appeared to have recruited marvellously by a winter's rest; when shabby loungers —oblivious to the fact that the sunshine brought out the grease spots and weak places of their apparel—basked in the sunshine and carried themselves as if a by-gone prosperity had come back to them. There were plenty of smart turn-outs to be seen, and daintily dressed ladies flitting from their carriages into shops, and gorgeous swells lounging to their clubs. Piccadilly looked so bright and gay, that it seemed as if the black cold drizzle of the London spring had grown into its short summer. No one on the pavement looked more gorgeous than

Colonel Beamish. No hat outshone his, no more splendidly blended trowsers could be seen, and no one had such a brand-new looking frock coat, or a more costly pin stuck into a more florid scarf. Looked at carefully, his face showed signs of constant brandy's and soda, and small bottles of champagne, taken perhaps to erase from his brain an ugly picture that always came across it. At first sight, he seemed prosperous and well content with himself and the rest of the world. So much so, that a shabby, down-at-heels looking man, who was as a matter of fact Cecil Warleigh's old comrade Flamby—took courage to greet him, and was rewarded for doing so by a luncheon, half a bottle of champagne, and the loan of ten shillings.

"Good-bye, Flamby, old lad," said Beamish, after the repast was finished and he had pleaded an important business engagement as a reason for getting away, "hope you'll have better luck this season. Back my colours when you see 'em, dear boy."

"Have you got any in training, then?" asked Flamby, wondering how Beamish managed to do it.

"No, but I shall have before very long, and I'll cut it pretty thick for 'em. I'll

make 'em a bit smart," answered Beamish,
and he swaggered down Regent Street,
Strandwards.

A stout white-haired gentleman—ex-
Inspector Sharp, dodged into the door-
way of a shop so as to let Beamish pass,
and then followed him across Leicester
Square, to Covent Garden, and then to
Burleigh Street, where he watched him
into a door-way. There were several
names written upon the walls within the
passage, but Inspector Sharp found it
easy enough to guess upon whom Beamish
was calling.

" Wonder where that ruffian has
sprung from ? Haven't seen anything of
him these six months. And what does
he want with Mr. Kit Lukes ? Sir Cecil
Warleigh stumped up like a man and a
gentleman ; but for all that, I can't help
remembering there is still a reward
out for you, and if Sir Cecil doesn't see
his way to doing anything else for me,
it might be worth my while to earn
it."

His thoughts were interrupted by the
driving up of a hansom, out of which
jumped the very man he was thinking of
—Sir Cecil Warleigh, who he noticed
wore a black tie and a band round his
hat. Mr. Sharp got on one side, so

as to let Warleigh pass without being seen by him.

"A warm lot—a dooced warm lot—Warleigh—Beamish and Kit Lukes," said Mr. Sharp to himself, as he lounged near the door. "I'd like to know what their game really is now."

Neither of the three gentlemen who were sitting round the table in Kit Lukes' office were just then in the very best of spirits.

"Sorry to say there's been a hitch, they want a more formal proof of the death. Pity you can't give it, Beamish. I understand you were present when the Basutos killed John Warleigh?" Kit Lukes was saying, eyeing Beamish malevolently out of his little blue eyes.

"Hang it, man, don't talk like that. I tell you I don't want to be mixed up in it. I was supposed to have been killed afterwards, and that's the end of me out there."

"Well, you know best, but I should have thought the mere crime of desertion from the Cape forces would not be likely to bring you into any great trouble now you have got back to England."

"Let's have no more of this d——d talk," said Cecil Warleigh, who began to look pale and worried, "if the money is not forthcoming yet, you'll have to wait for it. After all, it can't make much difference. You know it is sure to be all safe."

" It's very awkward for me, though, waiting ; I've got all my money in this thing, and haven't more than fifty pounds left out, to go on with. I want to be paid my money, and have done with it all," growled Beamish.

" And I would be glad enough to pay the money and have done with you," answered Cecil, looking, as he spoke, anywhere but in Beamish's face.

Just then there was a knock at the door, and a red-haired lawyer's clerk came into the office with a card in his hand.

" Two gentlemen to see Captain War- leigh, they say they must see him at once," the clerk repeated.

" Sir Cecil Warleigh, you mean, stupid," said Mr. Lukes, who generally bullied his subordinates.

" Yes, sir,—beg your pardon, sir, only Captain Warleigh was the name the gentleman said," answered the clerk.

" General Cottingham," said Cecil, as he took up the card. " Yes, he knew I was coming on here." Then he read another name written in pencil under

Cottingham. "Sir John Warleigh! Why, the General must have gone mad!"

"No, Cecil, my boy," said Cottingham, who had walked into the office, "it's a fact, Jack Warleigh has turned up again, fit and well, though his beauty is a little spoiled by a scoundrel of a trooper who tried to murder him. Look here, Cecil," he added in a lower voice, "it is hard luck on you, perhaps, but do the right thing, and say you are glad to see him."

Cecil stared blankly at the man who had followed Cottingham into the office. There was no doubt about it. He was Jack Warleigh. He looked much more of a man, harder and stronger. His face was disfigured by an ugly scar on the forehead, and his expression was a good deal altered from that of the easy-going, good-natured youngster whom Cecil had known.

"Yes, I thought the sooner you knew I had come back the better; and when Cottingham told me that you were here, I thought I'd come after you and let you know a piece of news that might influence the business you were about," said Jack Warleigh. Then he caught sight of Beamish, who, as soon as Jack had entered, picked up his hat and tried to slink out, without being observed.

" Hullo ! stop ! you infernal scoundrel. You and I have an account to settle. When the doctors in Cape Town operated on my skull the other week, and got up the splint of bone that was pressing on my brain, the first thing I remembered was your devilish face as I saw it when you were pointing your rifle at me. Cecil, what have you and this fellow got to do with each other ? "

Cecil Warleigh did not answer, his presence of mind seemed to have deserted him, and Cottingham, looking straight on, shrugged his shoulders, and began to suspect that Cecil had gone a little further than he, even in his most lenient moods, would be able to condone.

" What have we to do with one another ? Why, nothing at all, except that I owe him some money on account of some racing transactions," Cecil at last stammered out.

Beamish gave him a savage look, but said nothing, and made a rush to the door, getting through it, followed closely by Jack, who gripped him by the collar as they got into the passage.

" No, I am going to call a policeman and give you in charge for an attempted murder. I don't know much about the red tape of it, but I fancy they can try you here or elsewhere, for the shot you fired at me in Basutoland."

"You'll be sorry for it if you do. Cecil Warleigh and I are mixed up in this job together, as we have been mixed up in one or two other things. Unless you want to create an awkward bit of family scandal, you'll leave me alone. No, look here, Sir John, it's only fools who can't settle these affairs without bringing the peelers in."

"You scoundrel, do you think you are going to get off scot-free?" said Jack, keeping his grip on Beamish's collar, and looking out into the street for a policeman.

"Yes, that is just what I do think. You don't want to make an infernal story for every one to jaw about. Suppose you get a jury to believe I shot at you. Well, people would be asking themselves what my game was, and I would bring the man in who sent me out to do the job. Look at Cecil Warleigh's face, and guess who that was. Come, I am right, you ain't going to call a policeman, so don't make a fuss. It is a good bit easier to call in those gentlemen than it is to get rid of them afterwards."

Jack Warleigh looked from Beamish to Cecil, and he began to see that circumstances corroborated Beamish's charge.

After all, if that were true, the latter was the greater scoundrel of the two, and yet Jack felt that he would be sorry to see him charged with having compassed his death.

Beamish smiled pleasantly, feeling fairly confident that he would not have an embarrassing interview with a policeman. Jack realized that he had only two courses, either to let Beamish go about his business, or to invoke the aid of the law, and that might become embarrassing. Cecil Warleigh said nothing.

"It's an uncommonly awkward business," put in Cottingham, thinking how Cecil's disgrace would affect his daughter. The same thought came into Jack's mind, and that decided him, and he loosed his grip on Beamish's collar.

"Ah, I thought so, Sir John," said Beamish coolly. "May be, you and I will be able to do business together about a little information I can give you. For the present, good-bye!" and Beamish gave a tilt to his shiny hat, pulled a pair of loudly striped shirt cuffs over his wrists and swaggered down the passage. When he came to the door a stout, white-haired man with a soothing manner stood in his way, and tapping him gracefully on the shoulder said,—

"Stop a bit, Colonel Beamish alias Flash Dick. I arrest you for the old bank forgery business," then turning round to Cecil, he added, "Excuse me, sir, but I ain't a Scotland Yard man, and I ain't got no particular dooty to perform, except to myself—and if it is made worth my while —well—this gentleman can go free again."

Cecil shrugged his shoulders, it was nothing to him whether or no Beamish escaped.

Jack Warleigh was only too glad that justice should be done, and that the man who had tried to murder him should not go unpunished.

"Well, Colonel, our old score is to be settled," said ex-Inspector Sharp. "That was a nasty cowardly blow you caught me the last time we met. Still, 'all's well that ends well,' and a meeting like this, as the saying is, 'makes amends.' No, take it coolly, no violence, you don't catch me unawares twice, and there are a couple of real peelers this time who have the office. These gentlemen seem inclined to give you the cold shoulder, but when you have no other friend, you have me. I don't forget old times, or the fact that there is a reward offered for you," and as he spoke Mr. Sharp whistled, and two policemen, whom he had just before warned to be in readiness, appeared behind him, and in a trice Beamish was in their clutches.

"It's Flash Dick, a man who has been wanted any time these twenty-five years," said Mr. Sharp to the policemen. "I shall be able to identify him, all serene, when you get him to Bow Street."

Beamish didn't attempt an escape, but allowed himself to be marched off. Jack Warleigh looked at his watch, then jumped into a cab, as he wished to catch a train to Fetchester.

Cottingham went with him, anxious to avoid Cecil, whom he did not wish to talk to just then. The latter and Kit Lukes eyed each other in silence for a minute or two.

"I was a pretty well to-do man when I first met you, and now I haven't a fifty pound note in the world. That is what I've got by meddling in your affairs."

Cecil Warleigh experienced the second moment of satisfaction since Jack had appeared. The first was when Beamish had been taken into custody. Then remembering he had a balance of some hundred pounds at his bankers, and not feeling quite sure to whom, under the circumstances, that money might legally belong, he jumped into a hansom and drove off to draw a cheque for it.

Jack Warleigh had been brought down to Capetown as soon as peace had been patched up between the Cape Colony and the Basutos. A successful operation gave him back his memory and reason, and some days afterwards he was able to start for home.

At Capetown he saw Teddy Brigstock, who was going on well, and had been sent down to the coast.

The cable had broken down just then, as it was always doing in the first year of its existence, so Jack started off to bring to England the first news of his being alive and well again. The voyage home did wonders for him, and he arrived in England not much the worse in any respect, and in some a great deal better, for his stay in South Africa.

Arrived in London, he at once called upon General Cottingham, and from the General he heard that Cecil Warleigh had been with him a minute or two before, and had gone on to Kit Lukes'; "on a mission to raise money on the estates, I believe," the General added.

"Then I ought to let him know I have

come back," suggested Jack. "It would be only fair that he should know that at once."

"Don't know but that he'd sooner you wait till he had touched the money he was going to borrow," answered the General.

But Jack Warleigh had his way. And thus it happened that they turned up at Kit Lukes' office.

When the interview at the office was over, and Beamish had been marched off to Bow Street, Jack Warleigh drove to the station and just caught a train to Fetchester.

The quiet little town looked just as it did a year and a half before, when Jack last walked through its streets, and last startled the pigeons pecking about on the pavement outside the Swan Hotel. Jack felt that he was a good deal altered. He had grown stronger, and more of a man.

"No woman shall play the fool with me again," he declared to himself, as he remembered how bitterly he felt when he last visited the town of Fetchester. When he arrived near the gate of his mother's house, he waited for some time, remembering that his sudden appearance after he had been mourned for as dead, might be dangerous to his mother. As he waited there the front door was opened and a neat little figure came down the walk to the gate. It was Nelly Paradine. As she walked through the open gate-way she turned to the direction in which Jack was standing—but before she had time to recognize him he seized one of her little hands.

"Jack! dear Jack! Oh, you have come back to us! We all thought you were killed by the Kaffirs!" she cried, between her alternate bursts of sobbing and laughter. Then she told him of how they had mourned for him, and how she had come to be his mother's companion. "It has been a terrible time for her, but she will be well now," Nelly said. Then she turned and ran back to the house, where she broke the joyful news, while Jack waited outside.

Before Nelly had spoken many words of introduction to Mrs. Warleigh, that lady guessed the purport of her round-about address. So Nelly's news was anticipated before it was properly broken ; as it always is in such cases, be the news good or bad.

The widow's son had been given back to her again, and her husband's good name restored.

The next day, when Jack led Nelly up to her and told her that the old misunderstanding between them had been swept away, and the old troth-plight renewed, Mrs. Warleigh felt that after all Fate had been good to her, and that she had all she wished for. As to whether Jack would get his property and title back again, there seemed at first to be some slight doubt. But soon the legal difficulties that barred the way were got over, and on the second trial Jack Warleigh's case could not be resisted.

Before that event took place Colonel Beamish took leave for ever of his military title in the dock at the Old Bailey. He was tried and found guilty for being concerned in the bank forgery case, for which he had been " wanted " years before. It happened that the principal witnesses against him were still alive, and the case against him was perfectly conclusive. One of the first signs that he gave of his sentence to twenty years' penal servitude having had a beneficial effect on his morals, was to offer a full confession of the part he played in personating Captain John Warleigh, and in consequence he appeared in convict's garb on the second trial, and not only told his story on oath, but being confronted with the landlord and landlady of the Regent's Hotel, and some of the other witnesses, was able to convince them that he was the man who had married Sarah Matterson. Canon Bower's flock were somewhat shocked at the revelation of his youthful amusements which his evidence gave, but it proved Jack's case conclusively, and, to the credit of his parishioners as a body, it made him all the more popular and useful in his parish when it was realized that he had not shirked going into the witness-box.

The case was an evident certainty for Jack, and Cecil's counsel made but a pretence of fighting. Soon after the verdict was recorded against him, Cecil and his wife started for the continent, for a very prolonged tour. Cottingham's estimate of his daughter's strength of character was unhappily only too well founded. Her position—as the wife of a broken man, whose only income was an allowance which he received from Jack Warleigh, and what he could pick up at card tables and continental race-courses —was one which tried her too much, and the struggle she made against her difficulties was not a very determined one.

For a year or two she and Cecil lived

together, but for some time their married
life was not a very happy one. Then there
came a scandal and a row, which resulted
in Cecil Warleigh fighting a duel with a
Russian prince, in which he killed his
adversary. After this event, Kate and
Cecil parted, each going their own way.
The few people who ever offered an
apology or had a good word to say for
Cecil Warleigh declared that it was his
wife's conduct that broke him, and made
him so reckless and unprincipled. Kate
Warleigh never spoke to her husband
after that separation, and she only once
again saw him. It was on the pretty
little race-course at Florence. She was
on a drag, driven by Mr. Jabez P.
Shoddyman, and filled with that motley
following of ladies and gentlemen with
dubious foreign titles and soiled reputa-
tions, who settled on that enterprising
millionaire during his stay on the continent.

Kate Warleigh was looking at the
horses doing their preliminary before a
hurdle-race, and thinking somewhat
meanly of the jockeyship of the Italian
noblemen and officers, for it was a gentle-
men-riders' race.

"There is no countryman of Madame
Warleigh's riding," said a German baron,

" unless the rider of Prince Uffitzi's horse
is an Englishman. I think he rides like
one."

Kate's race glasses shook in her hand,
as the favourite came on to the course,
and galloped past the drag. Before she
saw the face of the rider, she knew the
figure and the way the rider sat his
horse. It was her husband. While the
competitors were waiting to be started,
Kate fixed her glance upon Cecil's face.
It was altered sadly for the worse. Late
hours and hard living had told their tale.
He was the only man she had ever cared
for, and she cared for him to the end.
As she watched him gallop his horse past
the stand, she thought of the old days,
when she was a girl—almost a child—
and he was a subaltern; and then a
bitter feeling of resentment came into her
heart, for she remembered how different
her life might have been if he had not
crossed her path. She did not watch the
race, only the one horse and its rider.
He was lying second at the last hurdle,
but as he took it the German officer,
riding the leading horse, came right
across him, and the two horses and their
riders went down together. Kate seemed
to know at once that Cecil was hurt.
The German was soon on his legs, and

the two horses were got up, but Cecil Warleigh lay quite still. Kate watched some men carry him away back to the stand. Presently one of their party, who had been away from the drag, came back with the news that the man who had had the ugly spill in the hurdle race was dead.

Kate kept very silent for some time, but by the last race she woke up again. Mr. Shoddyman had never found her so brilliant and attractive as on the drive home and at the dinner he gave to the party that evening, and when, after dinner and much champagne, he made her somewhat ambiguous proposals, he found that she was free to interpret them honourably, and they became engaged to be married a day or two afterwards. However, when he chanced to find out how recently she had become a widow when she accepted him, he felt rather shy of her, and incontinently fled back to the Western States. She was never married again, and is not likely to, for an attack of typhoid fever, caught in an Italian hotel, left her a crippled invalid. She is to be seen at watering places, wheeled about in a chair, and by her side her father, who has given up his beloved London and clubs for her sake.

Mr. Kit Lukes, having lost almost every penny he possessed in the world by the result of the case of Warleigh *versus* Warleigh, came to see that "honesty is the best policy." He made the discovery, however, too late in life to act on it, and in the following year his career was marked by his being "warned off" the turf, and struck off the Rolls. He is now clerk to an eminent member of the London criminal bar, and spends his time toadying thieves' friends for defences for his master. After Jack Warleigh married Nellie Paradine, he began to do his best to find something for his brother-in-law Sam ; and as he won a brilliant victory for the Government, signally defeating Lord Overbearing's candidate at the election, he had considerable interest with his party, and with the help of one or two of Sam's old Oxford friends who, now that he was not friendless, remembered him very well, managed to get him a post in the Heralds' Office, which he fills with dignity and comfort.

"'Pon my word, when I think of the past, and that it was I who brought that infernal fraudulent entry in the register to light, I feel ashamed to look you in the face," Sam said to Jack one evening, as they sat down to dinner at Warleigh.

"Yet, Sam," answered Jack, "in doing so, you were the best friend I ever had in my life, for I owe all that is best in it to the verdict in the first case of Warleigh *versus* Warleigh."

THE END.

www.ingramcontent.com/pod-product-compliance
Lightning Source LLC
Chambersburg PA
CBHW020845020726
47497CB00005B/1258